Enrollment Form

☐ **Yes!** I WANT TO BE A *Privileged Woman*.
Enclosed is one *PAGES & PRIVILEGES*™ Proof of
Purchase from any Harlequin or Silhouette book currently for
sale in stores (Proofs of Purchase are found on the back pages
of books) and the store cash register receipt. Please enroll me
in *PAGES & PRIVILEGES*™. Send my Welcome Kit and FREE
Gifts -- and activate my FREE benefits -- immediately.
More great gifts and benefits to come.

NAME (please print)

ADDRESS   APT. NO

CITY   STATE   ZIP/POSTAL CODE

PROOF OF PURCHASE ONLY

**NO CLUB!
NO COMMITMENT!**
*Just one purchase brings
you great Free Gifts and
Benefits!*

Please allow 6-8 weeks for delivery. Quantities are limited. We reserve the right to
substitute items. Enroll before October 31, 1995 and receive one full year of benefits.

Name of store where this book was purchased_____

Date of purchase_____

Type of store:

☐ Bookstore   ☐ Supermarket   ☐ Drugstore

☐ Dept. or discount store (e.g. K-Mart or Walmart)

☐ Other (specify)_____

Which Harlequin or Silhouette series do you usually read?

_____

Complete and mail with one Proof of Purchase and store receipt to:
U.S.: *PAGES & PRIVILEGES*™, P.O. Box 1960, Danbury, CT 06813-1960
Canada: *PAGES & PRIVILEGES*™, 49-6A The Donway West, P.O. 813,
North York, ON M3C 2E8

SIM-PP5B

▼ DETACH HERE AND MAIL TODAY! ▼

The deputy's green Jeep came to a stop beside her.

"Something wrong with your car?"

"Odd thing," she said, raising her eyebrows. "Suddenly my car overheated. One of the hoses worked loose."

"I'll give you a ride back to town, then Billy can come check it out," he answered.

"Thanks," she said, climbing inside.

He took off his Stetson and extended his hand to her. "My name's Derek Grey. I'm deputy sheriff assigned to Saddle."

She stared down at the strong, masculine fingers and wide palm. "I'm Alexandra Courtland...the doctor." His warm strong hand swallowed hers. He smiled, and the sexiest dimple she had ever seen appeared in his left cheek. Alex had the craziest urge to touch that charming dent.

Dear Reader,

We've got six more exciting books for you this month, so I won't waste any time before telling you all about them. First off, we've got *Caitlin's Guardian Angel*. This book represents a real milestone; it's the *fiftieth* Silhouette title by one of your favorite authors: Marie Ferrarella. It's also our Heartbreaker title for the month, and hero Graham Redhawk certainly lives up to his billing. You'll find yourself rooting for him in his custody battle for the adopted son he adores—and in his love for Caitlin Cassidy, the one woman he's never forgotten.

By now you know that our Spellbound titles are always a little bit different, and Lee Karr's *A Twist in Time* is no exception. Join forces with the hero and heroine as they journey into the past to investigate a murder whose solution is the only way to guarantee their own future. Laura Parker begins a new miniseries, Rogues' Gallery, with *Tiger in the Rain*. Years ago, Michaela Bellegarde brought Guy Matherson the best luck of his life. Now he's forced to turn to her once again—but this time, danger is on his trail. Leann Harris returns with *Trouble in Texas,* the story of a woman doctor "stranded" in a small Texas town. Love with the local sheriff is definitely the cure for what ails her, but, as so often happens, the road to recovery is not an easy one. Historical author Jessica Douglass makes her contemporary debut with *Montana Rogue,* a story of kidnapping, rescue—and romance. Don't miss it! Finally, welcome new author Amelia Autin. In *Gideon's Bride* she tells the story of a mail-order marriage threatened by the bride's deep, dark secret.

So sit back and enjoy all six of this month's Intimate Moments titles, then come back next month, when we bring you six more compellingly romantic books by some of the best writers in the business.

Yours,

Leslie Wainger
Senior Editor and Editorial Coordinator

Please address questions and book requests to:
Silhouette Reader Service
U.S.: 3010 Walden Ave., P.O. Box 1325, Buffalo, NY 14269
Canadian: P.O. Box 609, Fort Erie, Ont. L2A 5X3

TROUBLE IN TEXAS

LEANN HARRIS

Silhouette® INTIMATE™ MOMENTS®

Published by Silhouette Books

America's Publisher of Contemporary Romance

SILHOUETTE BOOKS

ISBN 0-373-07664-9

TROUBLE IN TEXAS

Books by Leann Harris

Silhouette Intimate Moments

Bride on the Run #516
Angel at Risk #618
Trouble in Texas #664

LEANN HARRIS

When Leann Harris first met her husband in college,
she never dreamed she would marry him. After all, he
was getting a Ph.D. in the one science she'd managed
to avoid—physics! So much for first impressions.
They have been happily married for twenty-one years.
After graduating from the University of Texas at
Austin, Leann taught math and science to deaf high
school students until the birth of her first child. It
wasn't until her youngest child started school that
Leann decided to fulfill a lifelong dream and began
writing. She presently lives in Plano, Texas, with her
husband and two children.

ACKNOWLEDGMENTS

I would like to thank the following people for their generous help: Dr. Robert Haley, Dr. Charles Haley, Dr. David Pate, Renee Swartz, R.N., Carol Patwari, R.N., and Sally Myers, R.N., for answering all my questions about TB.

Louisiana State Trooper Steven Barrett, for helping me think like a cop. Also, thanks for the insight into steroid abuse.

Lt. David Davis, who always answers my odd questions.

Deputy Jeff Carter, for helping with the organization of the Brewster County Sheriff's Department and the problems they face.

Nancy Glass, whose knowledge of Brewster and Presidio Counties, Alpine, Marfa and Marathon, cows and horses, and the flora and fauna of West Texas, was the most help I could ask of a friend and ex-roommate.

Chapter 1

"Is the Jeep ready?" Derek Grey asked as he strolled into the bay of the gas station.

"Yup," the mechanic answered, yanking the rag out of his back pocket and wiping his hands. "You want to see the new spark plugs I put in, Deputy?"

"No," Derek said with a sigh of exasperation. He'd grown up with Billy Mayer. But since he'd returned home to Saddle two years ago and taken the job of deputy sheriff, Billy had taken to calling him "Deputy."

The warning bell sounded, indicating a customer was at the pumps. Billy looked around the open hood of the Jeep and his mouth fell open. "Would you look at that?"

Derek glanced over his shoulder and the sight that greeted him made him feel as if he'd been hit by an angry bull, knocking the air from his lungs and the sense from his head. Standing beside a vintage red

Mustang was one of the most beautiful women he'd ever seen. She was short by most standards, but among the ladies in west Texas she was average height, maybe five foot four or five foot five. Her jeans and long-sleeved shirt, although modest, couldn't hide her shapely curves. Her strawberry blond mane was tied back with a ribbon, but wisps of hair danced around her face.

"I best ought to see what the lady wants." Billy hurried around Derek.

"Remember you're married," Derek said loud enough for his friend to hear.

Billy grinned and wagged his eyebrows. "But there ain't any harm lusting over the car."

Derek shook his head at his friend's behavior. He glanced again at the woman and all the male hormones in his body surged. "Quit acting like a teenager," he grumbled as he turned to inspect the work Billy had done. He chalked up his strong reaction to the woman to the fact that he'd been under a lot of stress lately with his daughter's flu and the endless complaints from ranchers about illegals on their land.

"May I help you?" Billy's voice floated into the garage.

"Yes, fill it with premium, please." The woman's voice was strong and clear, yet somehow it reminded Derek of the pure, musical notes of his mother's wind chimes. "I made the mistake of leaving Big Bend National Park without checking the fuel gauge."

"That's a deadly mistake out here, ma'am."

She laughed, a throaty sound that made Derek's blood heat in a way it hadn't since long before his divorce. Involuntarily, his attention was drawn from the spark plugs to the female standing by the old gas pump.

"I know better," she continued, "since I grew up in Midland. But having lived in Houston for the last eight years, I guess I forgot how far it is between gas stations out here." A frown marred her lovely face, and Derek wondered what had brought on the cloud of worry.

Billy lifted the nozzle on the pump. "Your car take unleaded?"

"Yes, it does. I had it converted several years ago."

He nodded and began to fill the Mustang with gas. The woman turned toward the station and must have caught sight of him, because her eyes widened in surprise. Caught staring red-handed, all Derek could do was nod, then go back to inspecting his engine.

"This is a mighty fine-looking car." Billy patted the trunk. "Is this a '65 or '66 model?"

"Sixty-six." The affection in her voice made Derek look up. She lightly ran her fingers over the fender as if the car held a wealth of memories. Oddly enough, Derek found himself envying the car.

"So you live in Houston? Do you like big-city life?" Billy asked.

Derek missed her reply.

"You work at a hospital?"

Silence answered the inquisitive mechanic.

"I saw the hospital parking sticker on the bumper," Billy explained hastily.

"Yes, I work at the county hospital."

"You a nurse?"

Derek smiled to himself. Billy Mayer had won the title of the nosiest human being in the county, and he was living up to his reputation.

"No, I'm a doctor."

"A doctor? You? Why, you're too pretty to be a doc."

Derek winced. In addition to being nosy, Billy was twenty years behind on social issues. Derek braced himself for the lady's comeback, sure she was fixing to tear a strip off Billy's tough hide. After a long silence Derek peered around the hood of the Jeep. The woman stood by her car, her hands clasped behind her back, her gaze locked on the horizon.

She turned to Billy. "Being ugly wasn't a prerequisite for medical school. Smarts were, but ugly wasn't."

A chuckle rumbled through Derek's chest. The lady had class, because instead of nailing Billy's hide to the door, she'd deflected his stupidity with humor.

"What kind of doc are you?" Billy wasn't fazed by her comeback.

"I'm an emergency room physician. You want a résumé?"

Billy laughed. "Naw. I'm just curious. We don't often get pretty d—uh—visitors through here."

She mumbled a reply.

"Since it's going to be several hours and hundreds of miles before you get to another gas station, let me make sure you've got enough water in your radiator and all the belts are in good shape."

"Thanks. I don't need to be stranded out in the middle of nowhere."

Something about Billy's offer bothered Derek. Billy was a good mechanic, but with this lady he was being too helpful. He gently put the hood down on the Jeep and walked out into the sunlight. The woman turned to him.

"Ma'am," Derek greeted her. He felt awkward and a little guilty for eavesdropping on the conversation, but he'd been in the garage before she drove up.

Her gaze traveled over him from head to toe, setting off every nerve ending in his body.

She nodded. "Sheriff."

The badge pinned to the shirt of his uniform must have given him away. "I'm a deputy sheriff."

The instant she addressed Derek, Billy straightened, banging his head on the hood. Flushing, he hastily slipped his screwdriver into his pants pocket.

"Everything okay under the hood, Billy?" Derek asked.

A flush crept up Billy's neck. "Looks good," he mumbled.

A nagging feeling gripped Derek as he watched the woman pay for her gas and drive off. The feeling was heightened when Billy hurried past him into the garage without a comment on the doctor or her car. Derek followed him into the dim interior.

"Did you do something to that lady's car, Billy?"

The mechanic jumped guiltily. "What makes you think that?"

"Your left eye is twitching. A sure sign you're up to something."

"I don't know what you're talking about. Your Jeep's ready."

Derek paid the bill and climbed into his vehicle.

"Uh, Derek," Billy called.

"Yes."

"You might want to drive north of town, just in case someone's stranded by the side of the road." Billy disappeared inside the building before Derek could question him further.

"Damn." The word exploded out of Derek's mouth as he hit the steering wheel with the palm of his hand. "I knew it. I knew Billy messed with that woman's car."

It was obvious to Derek why Billy had done what he'd done, only it wasn't right, no matter how good his intentions were. After Derek hauled the lady back to town, he was going to clean Billy's clock.

Alexandra slammed on the brakes, put the car into Park and glared at the red light on the instrument panel warning her the car was overheating. "I should've gotten a new, boring sedan," she complained, turning off the ignition, "instead of keeping a cranky, temperamental contraption like you that requires constant love and attention. You're worse than a husband."

Immediately Alex regretted her outburst. Her little Mustang had seen her through a lot. It was her first car. She'd been so proud of her purchase because she'd bought the car with money she earned, without help or money from her father. He'd railed when he'd seen the fourteen-year-old car, and told her he'd buy her a new Mustang. But Alex had remained firm.

For her, the car had been an act of validation, proof that she was worthy of people's respect and not just the spoiled daughter of a wealthy oilman.

Shaking off the old guilt, Alex got out of the car and rested her arms on the roof. In the distance the volcanic mountains stood nakedly against the endless blue sky. An ugly suspicion sprang to life. Her car had given her no trouble on the drive from Houston to Big Bend, then to Saddle. Why did the Mustang suddenly have problems? Had the mechanic done something to the car when he checked the engine? He'd acted jumpy when the deputy had called out to him.

Thinking back, Alex remembered the screwdriver Billy had hurriedly pocketed.

The suspicion sobered her. It showed her how her attitude toward people had changed over the past year. Before, she had always believed in the goodness of mankind. Not anymore. Not after the year she spent with the Red Cross in Bosnia; she'd seen firsthand what evil men were capable of doing.

Walking to the front of the car, she opened the hood and inspected the engine. Although she hadn't done the restoration of the Mustang, she had helped her high school boyfriend work on it, and she at least knew how to change the oil. The problem wasn't hard to find. A clamp holding a hose had worked itself loose and water was leaking from one end. She'd bet money that Billy had tampered with the clamp.

Her suspicions were strengthened when the deputy's green Jeep drove by, did a U-turn and came to a stop beside her. He rolled down the window and removed his mirrored sunglasses. Alex's stomach did a little flip as her gaze met his. Attraction, like the pull of the moon on the tides, flowed between them. She looked away, shaken by her reaction to this man.

"Something wrong with your car?"

As if you didn't know, she thought. "Odd thing," she said, raising her eyebrow, "suddenly my car overheated. One of the hoses worked itself loose."

She wanted him to act surprised, shake his head, click his tongue in sympathy, but he didn't. In fact, his dark brown eyes showed no reaction. "I'll give you a ride back to town, then Billy can come out here and check out your car."

Her mile-wide stubborn streak took control. She refused to go along meekly with this planned scam. "Thanks for the offer but I'll wait here with my car. I don't want anything to happen to it."

He glanced at the car, at her and then at the surrounding land. "Ma'am, it isn't safe for a lady like you out here. Not anymore."

"What do you mean?"

His expression hardened. "It means that I'm only one man and there are lots of miles in this part of the county that I can't cover. Things happen."

Alex didn't need him to enumerate the things. Numerous news stories had been done on the flow of people crossing illegally through Brewster and Presidio counties. The rising tide of violence because of drugs and weapons had the officials on both sides of the border worried. So it would be stupid for her to wait on the open road by herself.

"Your car can be replaced," he warned her. "Your life can't."

His eyes held hers, and she read the worry in their depths.

She nodded. "You're right, Deputy. It would be stupid for me to wait out here alone. And no one has ever accused me of being stupid."

"Or ugly." His mouth stretched into a tantalizing grin. The man was too handsome for her own good.

Alex's jaw fell open as she realized he was teasing her. Obviously he'd overheard her exchange with the mechanic.

He shrugged. "It was hard to ignore your conversation with Billy."

"You could've tried."

His eyes twinkled with amusement. "I was there first, if you'll remember. And of course, there's the basic law of physics—sound carries. What could I do?"

She started to laugh, then remembered she didn't trust this man. How did he know to come looking for her if he wasn't in on the scam?

After locking the car, Alex walked around the Jeep. Derek leaned across the bench seat and pushed open the door for her.

"Thanks," she said, climbing inside.

He took off his chocolate brown Stetson cowboy hat and extended his hand to her. "My name's Derek Grey. I'm the deputy sheriff assigned to Saddle, as you already know."

She stared down at the strong, masculine fingers and wide palm. "I'm Alexandra Courtland," she answered, "the doctor." His warm, strong hand swallowed hers. The contact of skin to skin sizzled through her, causing her heart to race.

He smiled, and the sexiest dimple she had ever seen appeared in his left cheek. Alex had the craziest urge to touch that charming dent.

He laughed, a deep rumbling sound that raised goose bumps on her arms. "It's a pleasure meeting you, even under these circumstances." He released her hand and put his cowboy hat on his head.

The attraction she felt for this man surprised and definitely annoyed her. He might be involved in something illegal, and she had no business being attracted to him.

"It was very fortunate for me that you drove by," Alex said as she buckled her seat belt. "Do many tourists get stranded out here?"

He slipped on the sunglasses. "No, not too often."

Of course, if he was in on the scam, he wouldn't admit such a thing to her.

As they drove back into town a tense silence settled around them. All of Alex's senses sprang to life and focused on the large male sitting beside her. He was a good-looking man with high cheekbones, a straight nose and generous mouth.

His Stetson hat covered wavy light brown hair but Alex remembered how a lock had fallen over one eye when he'd taken it off, giving him a certain disarming charm. Even if he hadn't been dressed in his uniform, Alex would've known he was an officer. There was something about the way he carried himself that said he was the law.

"Billy's a good mechanic. He should be able to fix your car."

"I certainly hope so." *Because he's probably the one who broke it,* she added silently.

As they drove up to the garage, Billy strolled out of the office, wiping his hands on a rag. The deputy stopped his Jeep in front of the mechanic and climbed out.

"The doc had trouble with her car a couple of miles down the road. Would you go out and see what the problem is?"

Billy never met the deputy's gaze. "Sure."

Alex scrambled out of the Jeep. "Do you need the ignition key?"

Billy shook his head. "No, I'll tow your car back here."

He didn't wait for a response but climbed into his tow truck and sped off.

The deputy shook his head, then turned to Alex. "It's going to take some time for Billy to fix your car. Why don't we go over to the diner and get something to eat while we're waiting?"

It was a reasonable suggestion. So why didn't she feel comfortable accepting it? Because she would have to spend more time with him, soaking up his masculine virility, that's why.

Alex opened her mouth to refuse but her stomach growled, loud enough for him to hear. He gave her a disarming smile.

"Your stomach agrees with me."

So did her hormones. Alex pursed her lips in frustration. "If I'm not here, how can I approve any repairs that need to be done?"

Derek looked down the single street that made up downtown Saddle. "He'll know where to find you."

Alex glanced at the signs on the few buildings. The post office, a feed store, a grocery store, Mabel's Diner, the sheriff's office and a small white building at the far end of the street that had no identifying marker. By the simple process of elimination, the diner would be the most logical place for her to be. "All right."

"Get in and I'll drive you to Mabel's."

Alex frowned at him. "But it's only a few feet."

"But if my Jeep's parked in front of Mabel's, Billy will know for sure where to find you."

Her streak of independence and stubbornness, which her father called damned unattractive and unfeminine, surfaced. "I'll meet you there. I need the exercise."

His eyes narrowed and she felt his gaze roam over her. "Doc, everything looks in good shape to me."

A mixture of outrage and unexpected, unwanted pleasure left her tongue-tied. With an abrupt nod she walked away.

Derek waited by the door to Mabel's for Alex to join him. He couldn't suppress a grin when he saw her prim expression. She was still miffed about his comment. She'd really be put out if she had any idea of the thoughts that had crossed his mind when he'd watched her shapely backside sway as she walked away from him.

He held the door open and waited for her to enter before him. She passed him without making a fuss about who should go first.

The usual lunchtime crowd, a couple of ranchers and several of their hired hands, was there. The instant Alex entered, all activity ceased. She froze, reminding Derek of a deer caught in headlights.

"What's going on out here, boys?" Mabel asked as she barreled out of the kitchen, balancing three plates on her arm. The instant Mabel saw Alex she stopped. "Well, I guess that answers my question." Mabel nodded to the table by the door. "Sit," she commanded the duo. After serving the men their lunch, Mabel grabbed two glasses of water.

Derek removed his hat and set it on the empty chair. As Mabel set down the glasses, Derek hurried to make the introductions. "Mabel, this is Dr. Alexandra Courtland. She had car trouble. Billy's looking at it now."

No one knew Mabel Vance's real age or her true hair color, but Mabel had the warmest heart in two counties and made the best peach cobbler in the state. The blue ribbons she'd won from the state fair hung on the wall by the front door, letting all know of her fame.

Throwing the towel in her hand over her shoulder, Mabel rested her fists on her hips. "So, you want two lunch specials?"

"What is the special?" Alex asked.

"Today it's chicken-fried steak."

Alex looked as if she'd sat on a whoopee cushion, with her eyes widening and her mouth forming an O. She cleared her throat. "Do you have anything else?"

"'Fraid not. It's Monday. Monday's chicken-fried steak. Tuesday's meat loaf. Wednesday's fried chicken."

Alex's thoughts were easy to read. Mabel's diner was cholesterol heaven or hell, depending on your view of the subject. But she smiled at Mabel and said, "Chicken-fried steak sounds wonderful."

Mabel nodded and disappeared into the kitchen.

Alex's actions surprised Derek. He had expected her to either turn up her nose at the fare or lecture Mabel on the dangers of frying.

"That was kind of you not to make a fuss," he told her.

She leaned forward. "I'll tell you a little secret." Her voice dropped to a dark whisper, making him think of lovers in the darkest hours of the night. "I love chicken-fried steak. With lots of cream gravy. And biscuits."

"What?"

She shrugged.

"But I thought all you medical types preached against such things as fat and cholesterol."

"Yes—well, an occasional fall from grace is permissible."

He liked this playful part of her personality. "Do you often fall from grace?"

The light dancing in her eyes instantly disappeared, to be replaced by a coldness that chilled him.

"Sometimes, Deputy, survival is the most important thing and nothing else matters."

What did chicken-fried steak have to do with survival? Derek wondered. Nothing, that's what.

Mabel reappeared at that moment with two plates of steaming food. "I've got cobbler when you finish with this. Just give me a holler."

Derek watched the doctor as she placed the first forkful of steak in her mouth. She chewed, then her eyes fluttered closed and her lips curved into a sensual line of satisfaction.

"Is it that good?" he asked.

"Heaven."

His imagination kicked into overdrive, and a vision played before his eyes of her lying across his bed, her blond hair fanning out around her head and that dreamy-eyed look directed at him. He swallowed hard.

"Is something wrong with your food?" she asked, concern coloring her husky, sensual voice.

Her question brought him back to earth with a jolt. "Everything's fine."

"Then why aren't you eating?"

She was one observant woman, he sourly admitted. "I was gauging your reaction."

"Oh, is that what you were doing?" The answer seemed innocent, but from the inflection in her voice he knew she suspected he'd been having erotic thoughts.

"Mabel," he called. "I need a cup of coffee." He turned to Alex. "Would you like some?"

She shook her head.

"Get it yourself, Derek," Mabel shouted back. "I'm busy."

After he got his coffee, the meal passed in relative quiet. He had just popped the last piece of biscuit into his mouth when she sprang her question.

"Why did Billy sabotage my car?"

The biscuit went down the wrong way and he choked. "What?" he gasped, reaching for his coffee.

"Why did he tamper with the clamp on the hose? Is he running some sort of a scam? Because if he is, I'll warn you that I'm not paying some outrageous price for the repair."

If she'd broken her plate over his head, he couldn't have been more surprised. "What makes you think Billy sabotaged your car?"

She gave him that cat-ate-the-canary smile. "The clamp on the water hose had been loosened. If it had been that way when I left Big Bend this morning, the car would've overheated long before I drove into Saddle."

Derek wanted to argue that Billy hadn't done it, but he was ninety-nine-percent certain she was right.

"Why did he do it?" Her eyes held his.

Mabel plunked two bowls of peach cobbler on the table, saving him from having to answer. "Here you go. Dessert." She gathered up the dirty dishes but didn't leave. "So, you're a doctor. It's good to see a woman doctoring." She gave Alex a conspiratorial smile. "Since we've been tending the sick since the Stone Age, we might as well get the credit. Men don't know squat."

Derek watched Alexandra bite back a smile.

"Isn't that so?" Mabel directed her question at Alex.

"Yes, it is," she answered.

Mabel nodded to Derek. "Now you take Derek, here. When his little Sarah was sick this winter, he didn't know a thermometer from a hot water bottle. He had to leave that little thing with his brother and his wife so she could get some proper tending."

He felt Alexandra studying him as if trying to read something hidden in his eyes.

"And you should've seen when Derek took—"

"Mabel, I need a refill on this coffee," Derek said, holding up his cup. He didn't want any more of the bitter brew, but he was desperate to shut Mabel up.

After giving him a pointed look, Mabel headed for the kitchen, her head held high.

Derek smiled weakly at Alex. "She tends to mother all the folks in the county," he explained.

"Maybe you need it." Alexandra took a bite of peach dessert. "You never did answer my question, Deputy."

Apparently the doc wasn't going to be diverted from her quest to know if Billy had rigged her car to overheat.

Mabel reappeared with a large coffeepot in her hand.

"What kind of doctor are you?" Mabel casually asked as she poured the coffee.

Derek silently moaned. It was beginning to sound as if the entire town was involved in a big conspiracy to pry into the doctor's life.

"I'm an emergency-room physician," Alex replied in an odd tone. The expression on her lovely face confirmed that she thought something fishy was going on in Saddle.

"You ain't interested in setting up practice here, are you?"

Derek's stomach sank to the floor.

"We've been without a doc since a year ago spring and this last winter it seemed like everyone got sick. Why, poor Norma, our postmistress, has been sick as a dog, lost weight and can't seem to shake her cough."

Alex gave Mabel a polite smile. "I'm on vacation from my job at Ben Taub Hospital in Houston." She opened her mouth to say something else but stopped.

Mabel shrugged. "Well, it was worth a try. If you need seconds on that cobbler, let me know."

The instant Mabel was out of earshot, the doc pierced him with a burning gaze. "There'd better be a good explanation for all this coincidence, Deputy, because, if there isn't, I'll report you to the attorney general's office."

Before Derek could answer, the restaurant door opened and Billy strolled inside.

"Good news," he said, stopping by the table. "All you need is a new water pump. Bad news is I'll have to send to El Paso to get it."

"And how long will that take?" the lady doctor asked carefully.

Derek braced himself for the fireworks.

"Two, maybe three days."

"That long?" Alex's voice was as chilly as the winter winds that whipped down from the mountains.

"There ain't many '66 Mustangs around here. I don't carry anything that would work in your car. But there's no cause to worry. I send to El Paso all the time. The bus brings it right to town."

"And how much is this going to cost me?"

Billy stared down at his hands. "Well, the thing is, I thought we could kinda trade services."

"What exactly do you have in mind?" The words fell from her lips like ice cubes, cold and firm.

"I'll fix your car in exchange for you looking at my mother-in-law. She's been sick for a while and needs some doctoring." Billy glanced at Alex. "What do you say?"

Hell, Derek grumbled under his breath. He should've known exactly what Billy was going to do. He just couldn't believe that his friend would deliberately damage this woman's car to keep her in town long enough to see his mother-in-law. But when people were desperate, they would do anything. He ought to know that after being a cop in San Antonio for nine years.

Alex closed her eyes and took a deep breath. "All right."

Billy beamed. "I'll just go call for that water pump. The deputy here can take you to the clinic. It's our pride and joy." Billy scrambled to his feet and hurried out the door without meeting Derek's disapproving gaze.

Alex stood and pushed in her chair. "Why don't you show me where this clinic is?" From the tilt of her chin Derek knew the doctor was angry.

"Okay." He reached for his hat, put it on, then led her onto the sidewalk. "This way." He started walking toward the last building on the street.

"Is there a phone in the clinic?" she asked.

He glanced over his shoulder at her. "Yes. Why?"

"After I check Billy's mother-in-law, I plan on making a call to Austin. Since the attorney general and

I are on a first-name basis, he might be interested in what's going on out here."

Derek stopped so suddenly she ran into his back. He turned and caught her before she fell. "And what exactly is going on out here?" His hands were clamped around her upper arms.

She jerked out of his grasp. "Oh, come on, Deputy, we both know what's happening."

He didn't like the direction of this conversation. "No, we don't. Why don't you tell me?"

"Why, you and Billy are running a scam, that's what."

With those thunderous and highly insulting words, she marched away.

Chapter 2

"Now, wait just a damn minute," Derek roared.

Before Alex could take another step, he snagged her arm and spun her around. From his expression, her accusation hadn't just made him mad; it had made him furious. She glared right back. Well, he wasn't the only one spitting mad.

"Are you saying I'm dirty?" he demanded.

She'd been the one who'd been railroaded into staying in this little town, then blackmailed into seeing a patient. And he was acting as if he was the victim. "If the shoe fits..."

His eyes narrowed, giving him a predatory look. With that expression Derek Grey could've passed for one of the gunslingers who roamed Texas a hundred years ago.

"Well, it doesn't," he snapped. "I've been a law officer for over eleven years and no one has ever accused me of so much as fixing a traffic ticket. I pay my taxes and bust my butt to make this part of the world safe. And all I get for my effort is the federal government jumping down my throat about illegals, the border patrol making power plays and the governor standing on her head about my hiring practices when this town can barely afford to employ me. And you think I'm dirty?''

Apparently she'd touched a raw spot. "Well, if they don't pay you enough—''

"Don't even finish that," he warned in a low, deadly voice. He glanced into the window of the feed store. She followed his gaze and saw an audience staring at them. The two men and one woman looked from her to the deputy. Derek grabbed her arm. "Come on. I don't fancy having any observers to this conversation."

Neither did she until she knew whose side these observers were on. Alex allowed him to guide her toward the small white building at the end of the street. Once they were close enough, she saw the plain metal plaque screwed into the wall by the front door: Brewster Clinic. Immediately something inside Alex shrank back. She didn't want to go inside.

"If you grew up in Midland," he said, holding open the door for her, "then you ought to know that honor is still a way of life out here in this part of Texas."

Alex wanted to turn and go back to the restaurant, but then she'd have to explain her odd reaction. And she wasn't in the mood to explain anything to anybody. She brushed past him, and the warmth of his large body seemed to wrap around her and draw her to him. His heat was a welcome relief to her battered psyche.

She glanced around the neat, modestly furnished waiting room. "Is that what you label Billy's actions, honorable?"

That brought Derek up short. He sighed and the sound went bone deep. "No." He rubbed the back of his neck. "What Billy did was wrong." He strolled over to a green chair and sat down. "I should've known what he was doing when he started questioning you. But Billy's always been a snoop, and I just assumed he was being his own nosy self."

"And when did you suspect him of tampering with my car?"

"The instant you left. Billy has this little twitch in his left eye that kicks in when he's done something wrong."

"Really?" Alex folded her arms beneath her breasts. She wanted to believe him, but over the past twelve months she'd seen too much violence, seen too many men lie and break their word, to allow her that luxury.

"Yes. First time Billy and I smoked a cigarette in the boys' bathroom, Mrs. Byers caught us. I think I could've convinced her that we didn't do it, but Billy's tic gave us away."

He'd just admitted he'd lied as a youth.

"Don't give me that look, lady. I'll lay odds you didn't make it through adolescence without lying."

She hadn't, but she wasn't going to admit that to him. Besides, she had her own sins to worry about.

"That cigarette made me sicker than a dog and I never touched another one. The whipping my dad gave me added immensely to my dislike of smoking."

A smile crept up on her. "Your dad sounds as tough as mine."

He shrugged. "I'm sorry about Billy. The guy's worried to death about his mother-in-law. It doesn't excuse his actions, but maybe you can understand why he did it."

The sheriff seemed honest and his story reasonable. But then again, some of the zealots she'd encountered this past year had seemed honest. Besides, she wasn't ready to deal with patients just yet. She was emotionally drained and didn't want to get involved with anyone's problems. "His stunt could've ruined my car's engine."

"Yes, it could have," he agreed. "It was a stupid thing to do."

"He's lucky I pay attention to my panel lights and stopped when the temperature light came on."

"He is," he calmly answered, his voice a comforting tone.

She didn't want him to agree with her. She wanted to hold on to her righteous anger because it would protect her, but he was being too reasonable. "So what am I going to do for two days after I examine Billy's mother-in-law?"

"You could visit my family's ranch and play cowgirl."

Alex laughed. "Deputy, when I was growing up, I saw the back end of more cattle than I wanted to. Since I left Midland, not once has the urge to see a cow overwhelmed me."

He flashed her a brilliant smile. "It's that or spend the time looking at me."

That thought terrified her more than punching cows. Cows weren't a threat, but this man might be . . . one way or another.

* * *

"Come on, Mom. The doctor says she's willing to have a look at you," Billy said as he ushered a tiny woman into the clinic.

"And why did she agree to do that?"

Billy stopped and glanced at Norma. His left eye twitched. "Because she's a nice lady."

Norma placed her fists on her hips but her frosty pose was ruined by a hacking cough.

Billy slipped his arm around her waist. "Are you all right?"

She waved him away. "You're not going to get away without answering my question. Your eye's twitching, a sure sign something's up."

Derek glanced at Alexandra. She was observing the little drama playing itself out in front of her. Her expression gave no clue as to what she was thinking. But Billy's argument with Norma was an independent confirmation of Derek's explanation.

"Now, Mom."

"Don't 'now' me. Why is this woman doing this?"

Alex stepped forward. "Your son-in-law told me you were sick, and I couldn't see letting this delay go to waste."

Norma eyed the stranger. "That doesn't explain why Billy's eye's twitching."

A calculating light entered the lady doctor's eyes. "I plan to examine Billy later, believe me. But for now, why don't we go into the examining room and let me check you out."

The older woman hesitated. "Are you sure?"

"Positive," Alex replied, giving Norma an encouraging smile. Her warm, welcoming action seemed to ease the stiffness in Norma's spine. Derek marveled at the change in the lady doctor. She'd gone from a suspicious investigator to a reassuring medical professional.

Derek waited until the women were in the other room before he turned to Billy. "You're in lots of trouble, buddy."

Billy slumped down into a chair. "Yeah, I guess I screwed up big time."

"What the hell possessed you to do that?"

"She's a doctor. I thought that maybe if she saw the clinic she might—" He propped his elbows on his knees and hung his head. "Aw, I don't know what I thought. Norma's been sick too long. She needed to see a doctor. I've tried all winter to get her to drive over to Alpine and see a doctor, but she said she couldn't afford the time away from her job as postmistress." Billy picked at the nonexistent crease in his work pants. "Since Doc Talbot retired and moved to Florida, Norma's refused to see any doc."

"Maybe's she nervous about seeing a stranger. Doc Talbot was here for thirty years."

Billy tapped his heel on the floor, a sign of nervousness that often accompanied his eye-twitching. "I guess."

Derek listened to the tapping for several moments, trying to decide the best way to say what he needed to say. "Billy."

"Yeah."

"Some folks might consider what you did to Dr. Courtland's car illegal. The county D.A. would consider it criminal mischief."

"I'm not going to charge her for repairs," Billy replied, sitting up straight.

"That's a moot point. What you did was wrong. If the lady doctor wants to press charges, she's got every right."

"You can't tell me you weren't worried about your daughter when she had the flu."

"Of course I was, but I didn't snatch a doctor off the road and hold her car hostage."

Billy mumbled an incoherent answer. A frown creased the mechanic's brow. "You think the doc will press charges?"

"She was pretty mad about what you did," Derek answered truthfully.

"Could you talk her out of it?" Billy sounded like a hopeful little boy.

"I shouldn't try."

"Come on, Derek. Would you do this for your best friend?"

What Billy was asking him to do was excuse his criminal behavior. Billy was arguing that the circumstances justified his actions. "I can't do that."

Billy shook his head. "I didn't think you could. You know, since your divorce, you've become a pompous ass."

Didn't he know it.

Alex tried to keep her expression pleasant and neutral, ignoring the deep concern tightening her stomach. Opening the patient file that Dr. Talbot had kept on Norma Bolton, she scanned it looking for the last recorded weight.

"You've lost some weight, haven't you, Norma?"

"About twenty pounds, but it was all weight I could spare." She coughed into a tissue. When the spasm passed, she smiled weakly at Alex. "It's been a hard way to lose it."

Norma had all the classic symptoms. A persistent deep cough, fever, night sweats, lack of appetite, weight loss, fatigue. All these symptoms had lasted for months.

"Well, what's your opinion, doc? What do I have? It's bronchitis, right? Doc Talbot told me to stop smoking, but it's the one vice I allow myself."

Now wasn't the time to panic Norma. That could come later. "It could be bronchitis, but it might be something else. A fungus, asthma. I'll need to run a couple of tests to be able to make a correct diagnosis."

"What kind of tests?"

Here's where the rubber met the road. "I'll need to do what's called a PPD test." Alex waited for Norma's reaction. If she knew what the test was used for, she might become alarmed.

"What's that?"

No panic. Things were progressing well. "PPD is short for purified protein derivative. I inject this protein under the skin on the inside of your forearm. Then we wait seventy-two hours and see how your body reacts to the test."

"Can you do it here?"

"Yes, if there's a PPD test available. If there isn't, then I'll have to send to the nearest hospital for one."

Norma quietly studied her. "What's this test for?"

Alex closed the folder and laid it on the counter behind her. "It's just a precaution. To eliminate some of the far-out possibilities."

"Name me one."

Rats, Alex silently said to herself. She'd hoped to get away without telling Norma what she suspected. The people out here in west Texas were tough, independent and wanted reasons for everything. "Tuberculosis."

All the color, which wasn't much, drained from the older woman's face. Her eyes went black with fright. Alex grasped Norma's hand and rubbed it.

"Listen to me, Norma. This is only a possibility."

"Then what makes you think I have it?"

It was like walking a tightrope, trying to get Norma to allow the test, yet keeping her calm. Alex couldn't tell Norma that she recognized the combination of symptoms because she'd seen them with more and more frequency over the past years. TB was a rising problem with the poor and homeless population that Alex dealt with at the charity hospital. "You have some of the symptoms and I wanted to rule it out."

"I remember my grandmother talking about friends who died of TB."

"Today, TB is not a death warrant. If, and I stress *if,* you have it, you'll be on several medications for a year. If you finish the prescribed therapy, there's no reason you won't recover."

Norma clasped her ink-stained fingers tightly. "You know, Dr. Courtland, I'm not the only one who's been sick this winter. Do you suppose that maybe I'm not the only one with this?"

A sick dread squeezed Alex's heart. "Norma, we don't know if *you* have TB. Let's just tackle one thing at a time."

Derek and Billy frowned at each other at the noise that came from the examining room. It sounded like the slamming of a door. It happened several times in a row.

"What's going on in there?" Billy asked.

"The doc's looking for something. Maybe I ought to go see if I can help her."

"Do that," Billy agreed.

Derek had just stepped into the hallway when Alex and Norma emerged from the small room.

"Everything okay?" he asked. "Billy and I heard slamming doors and wondered what was happening."

Alexandra's eyes bored into his. "I was looking for a PPD test to give Norma."

Shock held him in place for a moment. He knew what PPD tests were used for. He'd been tested a couple of years ago when a homeless man he'd collared for breaking into a business had been diagnosed with active TB. He cleared his throat. "Did you find one?"

"No. I'll need to call the nearest hospital and get one." Alexandra's voice was calm, and he was grateful for her composed attitude. He wondered if Norma knew what the test was used for.

Billy walked to his mother-in-law's side. "How are you?"

"I don't know. Dr. Courtland needs to do some tests."

Billy frowned. "What kind of tests? Why can't she just tell you what's wrong with you? Doc Talbot could've." Billy directed his words at Alexandra. "What kind of doctor are you?"

"Billy," Norma protested.

"Well, it's true," Billy replied, defending himself.

"Then next time," Alexandra said in a cold tone, "you'll have to be more selective in the doctor whose car you hijack."

"What?" Norma said, turning to her son-in-law. "What did you do?"

Alex grasped Norma's hand. "Don't worry about it. All we need to do is discover what's wrong with you."

It was obvious from her reaction that the lady doctor could handle herself, but a protective instinct sprang to life in Derek. What was wrong with his friend to jump all over Alexandra the way he had? Reining in his deep anger so he wouldn't sound like a raving idiot, he growled, "Billy, I believe you owe the lady an apology. Then afterward, you can take Norma home."

A dull red stain crept up the mechanic's neck. His foot kicked some imaginary object on the floor. "I'm sorry. Sometimes my mouth works before my brain gets into gear."

"Try 'always,'" Derek mumbled to himself.

The corner of Alex's mouth twitched, and he guessed she'd overheard his remark. Well, the lady deserved a little laugh after the day she'd had in Saddle.

Norma gave the doctor an apologetic smile. "I'll be at the post office until five. Then home. Call me when you need me."

"Norma, you'll need to find someone to take over your job at the post office. Until we know what you have, it isn't wise for you to be in contact with others. Go home and rest."

Norma's lips pressed into a grim line. She nodded, then walked out of the clinic.

Billy frowned as he watched Norma leave. He glanced at Derek, then Alex. "What's going on?"

"Why don't you see if you can help Norma," Derek answered.

It looked as if Billy wanted to argue but Derek folded his arms across his chest, silently telling Billy he wasn't going to get any more information. His friend got the message and left without another word.

Derek waited a moment before turning to Alexandra. "Pay no attention to Billy. He's got as much sense as a gnat." He thought for a moment, then added, "Maybe less."

She shrugged. "I've run into several men with attitudes similar to his." Her eyes clouded and her mouth compressed into a tight line. She shook off the odd melancholy. "But Billy's attitude is not the problem. It's Norma. I think she has an active case of tuberculosis. And if she does, then we're going to need to start checking others. Her family is the first group that needs to be tested."

"What makes you think it's TB? It's such an unusual diagnosis, especially out here."

She rounded on him. "Are you going to question my qualifications, too? Does my being a woman somehow make my judgment of less value than a man's?" She stood with her fists on her hips, chin out in a challenging tilt.

Derek thought he'd just asked a simple question. But from her violent response he decided something else was going on besides his asking about TB. He held up his hands in mock surrender. "Hey, this has nothing to do with your judgment or your sex. I can't fault either."

It was the wrong thing to say because her blue eyes went dark with anger. "My sex?"

"Whoa, lady. Don't jump to any conclusions."

Her shoulders relaxed and her hands left her hips. "All right, I'm listening. Please explain what you meant."

"What I meant was how did you come to the conclusion Norma has TB? I mean, it's not the top disease on everyone's list. It's kind of unusual, you must admit. But it was rampant in my grandmother's youth, not today."

She closed her eyes and rubbed her forehead, and Derek had the impression that the weight of the world rested on her slender shoulders.

"I'm sorry I overreacted," she said. "I've seen too much of the bad side of humanity lately. I just assumed the worst."

He wondered what she'd been through that had made her so defensive and suspicious. Of course, he couldn't point any fingers after his years on the street as a cop and his bitter divorce two years ago. Yeah, he could identify with being cynical. "No problem."

A frown creased her brow. "But it is. When you stop trusting people . . ."

Her shoulders slumped and Derek wanted to wrap his arm around her slender form and draw her close. But if he succumbed to that impulse, it would only lead to disaster. He had the feeling that if he laid a finger on her, she'd smack him. Not that it wouldn't be worth it, but he didn't want to add a physical confrontation to the indignities she had already endured. Still, he was tempted.

"You asked about the TB."

Her voice brought him out of his mental wanderings and he hoped none of his thoughts showed on his face.

"In Houston I worked with the indigent population where TB is a rising problem. Norma has all the classic symptoms. I ruled out asthma, because she didn't respond to the inhaled medicine. Bronchitis wouldn't have acted the way this has over time. Now, it could be a fungus she picked up or lung cancer since she's a smoker, but I've got this gut feeling..." She fell silent and gave him a look that was equal parts embarrassment and need for him to understand.

"Being a cop, I understand gut feelings. It's saved my bu—backside more than once."

She grinned and glanced down at the part of his anatomy he'd mentioned. He felt that gaze like a gentle caress and his body reacted immediately.

"Don't look so shocked," she told him, humor lacing her words. "Women look."

He wanted to tell her he'd done some looking of his own, but wisely decided not to mention it.

"But there's one thing that's bothering me. Out here in the open spaces it's unusual that she'd be exposed long enough to catch TB."

"She who?" Derek asked.

"Norma." Alexandra graced him with a look that said, *Why can't you follow a simple conversation?* He could if it was linear. This one wasn't.

She bit her bottom lip and Derek's gaze was riveted on the action. What would it be like—

"Norma's the postmistress, right?"

His hormones were clouding his brain function. "Yes," he finally managed to answer.

She walked to the window and looked down the street. "What does the post office look like?"

Was he missing something here? "Four walls and a roof. Why?"

It was as if someone had put a steel rod in her spine. "What kind of walls? How old is the building? What kind of lighting does it have?"

"Why is that important?"

She turned and crossed her arms. The action drew her shirt tight over her breasts. She was the best-looking doc he'd ever seen.

"Because, Deputy, that could be the key to this mystery. If the post office is small, dark and poorly ventilated, then Norma having TB would make sense."

He gave her a puzzled frown.

"To catch TB you have to be exposed to it over time. Small enclosed places are breeding grounds for TB bacillus."

The seriousness of the situation hit home and Derek swallowed hard. "I hope that there's another explanation."

"Why?"

"Because my daughter spends her afternoons with Norma after she gets out of school."

Chapter 3

After calling the hospital in Alpine to make sure they had the PPD tests, Derek arranged for his daughter, Sarah, to stay with Mabel until he got back, which would be close to midnight.

The drive to the hospital passed in total silence. Alex knew that the deputy sheriff was worried about his daughter. He had a right to be. After seeing the post office she was even more convinced that what they were dealing with was TB.

The building was a hundred-year-old landmark. The stone had come from the Davis Mountains to the west, brought to Saddle on the backs of donkeys. The ventilation was poor and the direct sunlight minimal. It was a textbook example of the breeding ground for TB bacteria. And if Derek's daughter spent two to four hours daily in that building with Norma, chances were the twelve-year-old also had tuberculosis.

The thought upset Alex. After all the suffering she'd
seen in Bosnia—the death, the wanton wounding and
raping—a numbness had encased her soul that had
lasted months. Yet concern for Sarah Grey's plight
had broken through that indifference, which surprised her.

It also confused her. After three years working in
the emergency room at Ben Taub, dealing with the
tragedies that occurred in a big city like Houston, then
the time in Bosnia, Alex wasn't sure there was anything left in her to give to patients.

She admitted to herself that it had been unwise for
her to immediately return to Ben Taub. That first
morning, ten minutes into her shift, a shooting victim
had been wheeled in and she'd discovered she couldn't
handle the feelings and visions that swamped her. After that, she had decided to quit medicine altogether,
but her boss, Everett Carlin, had talked her into taking a month's vacation before doing anything rash.

And that's how she managed to be out in west
Texas. An old high school friend had married a park
ranger in Big Bend National Park and Alex had spent
the past month enjoying the wild beauty of the Chi-
sos Mountains. But she was no closer to knowing what
to do with her life than the day she left Houston.

"There's the hospital," Derek said, pointing to the
white stucco building at the foot of the mountains. He
whipped his Jeep into a tight parking space and turned
off the ignition.

Alex took a deep breath to calm her racing heart as
she glanced at the hospital. She could do this, she
sternly told herself. But the instant she stepped
through the hospital doors, a sense of panic gripped

her. She wanted to turn and run into the cool evening air.

"Are you all right?"

Derek's deep voice broke through her anxiety. She glanced up into his handsome face and saw concern.

"I'm fine," she said, pasting a smile on her face.

"You sure?" The man was too perceptive. It would be hard to hide secrets from him, if she had any.

"Who's the doctor here?" she asked, trying to divert his attention from her reaction.

"You are," he calmly replied, "but I'm the peace officer and can smell a falsehood a mile off."

Great, a cop with a minor in psychology. "Shouldn't we see about the tests?"

He hesitated, then nodded. After checking with the receptionist for directions, they made their way to Dr. John Shelly's office.

As they walked down the hall, the familiar smell, the clatter of dishes as the attendant served dinner to the patients, the voices floating out of the rooms pressed in on Alex, smothering her. She didn't want to be here.

The head of county health stood outside his office. He glanced at his watch. "I've been waiting for over an hour for you two to show up. I've got to drive over to Marfa and see a patient." He motioned them inside.

Alex and Derek exchanged a glance. His said, *I told you so,* which he had. After Alex had talked to the youthful doctor on the phone, Derek had told her that Dr. Shelly was a good physician, but he wouldn't win any congeniality awards.

The instant they were seated, Dr. Shelly launched into his questions.

"Why do you think this woman has TB?" His tone was filled with doubt.

It was a familiar routine for Alex, to defend her diagnosis to a male counterpart. Only today Alex wasn't in the mood to be polite and accommodating.

"She has all the classic symptoms. If you think I'm way off the mark, then I suggest you drive to Saddle yourself and examine Norma. And if you doubt my skill as a diagnostician, call Dr. Everett Carlin at Ben Taub Hospital. He'll vouch for me."

Dr. Shelly straightened his shoulders. "Since I have responsibilities here, I am unable to travel to Saddle. But I'll be happy to supply you with the tests."

He stood and walked around his desk. "How many do you need?"

She glanced at Derek. "How many do you think? Norma, her family, your daughter. Is there anyone else?"

Derek rubbed the back of his neck. "Damn. Everyone hangs out around the post office. It's the social center of the town. Since there is no rural delivery, everyone comes into town for their mail. Sometimes folks can only get in once a week or once every other week. Then they stay and talk, find out what's been going on."

The situation in Saddle was looking grimmer and grimmer. The little town in west Texas might make news in medical journals: TB Epidemic In West Texas.

"How many tests do you want?" Dr. Shelly asked again.

They didn't need to panic yet. First they needed concrete evidence that Norma was infected. She looked at Derek. "Would you say ten tests? That will give me more than I need."

"Sounds fine to me," Derek replied.

She turned back to Dr. Shelly. "If Norma comes up positive, you'll need to send tests for the entire population of the town, as well as someone to administer them and follow up."

"Oh? Won't you be there?" Dr. Shelly asked, his nasal tones as annoying as fingernails on a chalkboard.

"Dr. Shelly, as you well know, I am not this town's doctor. I was driving through Saddle, going home from my vacation, when my car broke down." She threw a meaningful look at the deputy. "While I waited to have it fixed, I was asked to examine Norma. As soon as my Mustang is fixed, I plan to go home."

Her words could be interpreted as heartless and uncaring, but she couldn't help that.

"You will stay the seventy-two hours it takes for this first test to be complete, of course."

Dr. Shelly's superior attitude was obnoxious and totally out of line. The man made it sound as if she was the one delinquent in her responsibility. She had no legal obligation here, but unfortunately she couldn't ignore the moral and ethical obligation. "Yes, I'll stay to read Norma's test."

He nodded and left the room.

"I'm sorry about this," Derek said.

She shrugged.

"I know Billy didn't mean for you to have to stay in Saddle for three days."

She shifted in her chair, turning toward the deputy. "Really? From what I saw of your well-equipped clinic, it appears you were looking for a doctor. One who was going to stay."

He dropped his gaze to his hands. "I'll admit that the town council has been searching for a doctor. We've tried everything to lure one out here. We've gone to medical schools and talked to the graduating students, offering them attractive contracts. We've gone to medical conventions, placed ads in medical journals, beat every bush we could. So far, we've not had one interested applicant."

"So Billy just decided to hijack one."

Derek flushed. "Billy wasn't thinking. I'm sorry."

"I'm sorry, too." And sad and confused. Apparently the part of her soul that cared about others hadn't completely died. And although she didn't know if she wanted to continue practicing medicine, she couldn't walk away from this situation. She prayed that she was wrong about Norma, because if she wasn't, she could be in a heap of trouble.

"I want to go by the sheriff's office and check on a couple of things," Derek said as they walked out of the doctor's office.

"Sure," Alex absently responded, making Derek wonder if she was even aware she'd answered him.

Derek glanced at the beautiful woman by his side. The harsh hospital lights didn't dim her natural beauty. Derek's gaze slid down her slender but shapely figure. She might be a good ten inches shorter than him, but he bet that her curves would fit perfectly into the planes of his body.

A small frown had settled between her arched brows and she seemed lost in thought. *What was bothering this lady,* he wondered, because sure as rattlers have fangs, the doctor was hiding something.

The cool night air rushed around them as they exited the hospital. As they drove downtown to the town square where the sheriff's office was located, Derek looked at the surrounding mountains and felt that sense of belonging that had brought him back to this land. When he turned off the Jeep's ignition, Alex threw him a puzzled look. "Why are we stopping?" She glanced around. "And where are we?"

He shook his head and climbed out of the Jeep. "I told you."

"When?" she called after him, scrambling out of the vehicle.

"When we were at the hospital. I told you I needed to talk to my boss." Derek held the door to the sheriff's office and waited for her to enter before him.

The young man seated behind the desk rose to his feet. "May I help you, ma'am?"

"She's with me, Nick," Derek answered, strolling to Alex's side.

The young man's gaze moved from Alex to Derek.

"Derek, what are you doing here?" he asked.

"It's been so long since I've seen your face, Nick, I decided I needed to check and make sure you were as ugly as I remember."

"If you wanted to see ugly, all you had to do was look in the mirror," the young man replied. "Are you going to introduce me to the lady?"

"Nick, this is Dr. Alexandra Courtland. Alex, this big gorilla is Nick McFarland."

"A doc. She's a doctor? Why, she's too—"

"Don't say it, Nick," Derek warned.

A puzzled expression settled on Nick's face. "Why? I was just going to say how pretty she is."

Alex held out her hand. "It's a pleasure, Deputy McFarland."

The admiration in the younger man's eyes shone as his gaze moved over Alex's face and down her body. "The pleasure is mine," Nick gushed, shaking her hand.

For an odd moment Derek wanted to knock Nick on the side of the head and tell him to quit salivating. "Is Wes here or has he already gone home?"

"He's in his office, going over some information the DEA gave him."

Just then the door on the opposite wall opened and a tall man with a head of silver hair and a salt-and-pepper handlebar mustache emerged. "Derek, you must be psychic. You're just the man I needed to see." He stopped and looked at Alex. "I'm Wesley Clayton, ma'am, sheriff of this county. And you're?"

"Dr. Alexandra Courtland."

The sheriff stuck out his hand, and Alex's small hand was swallowed up in his larger, tanned one. "It's a pleasure, doctor. Are you new in town?"

Alex glanced at Derek. *Should I tell him the truth?* she asked silently.

He shrugged.

She turned back to the sheriff. "My car broke down just outside of Saddle."

"And Billy couldn't fix it?"

"He's repairing it now."

"He'll do a good job." The sheriff ran his fingers over his mustache, then cleared his throat. "If you'll excuse us, ma'am, I need to talk to Derek. Nick, why don't you get Dr. Courtland a cup of coffee or one of those soda drinks you like?" Wes motioned Derek into his office. Once the door was closed behind them, he turned and leaned against the desk. "The DEA guys called me this afternoon. Last night they observed a low-flying plane crossing into the county." Crossing his arms across his wide chest, Wes rubbed his chin. "This is the third time this month they've spotted a plane coming into the county. They lost track of the plane around Split-Tree Rock."

"That's not that far from my family's ranch."

"That's why I needed to talk to you. DEA wants to use your ranch as a base of operation to do some nighttime reconnaissance in that area. They're going to be looking for a landing strip or any sign of smuggling."

That's just what Derek needed at the moment, a smuggling ring operating in his backyard. "When do they want to set up?"

Wes stared down at his boots. "They wanted to drive out there tomorrow."

The headache developing behind Derek's eyes was turning out to be a real killer. "Leave it to the feds to want everything yesterday. Now, if you want something from them, it's another story."

"Generally, but you've got to admit Chuck's not a bad guy. He's worked to improve the relationship between the locals and the feds."

A disgruntled sound erupted from Derek's throat. "I'll have to check with my brother, since he and his wife are the ones who will have to put up with those guys, but I don't think it will be a problem."

"Good. Now, tell me who Alexandra Courtland is and why you two are here in Alpine if her car played out in Saddle?"

If Derek was facing the medical crisis he thought he was, Wes needed to know the situation. Derek quickly explained.

"TB, damn." Wes gave a low whistle. "If it turns out to be that, you know I'll do everything I can to help."

"Thanks, Wes. I knew I could count on you."

As Derek pulled open the office door, and he and Wes joined the others, he heard Alex ask, "So your dad was a Texas Ranger?"

Beaming, the young man answered, "Yes, ma'am. He was a captain when he retired last year. I'm the third-generation peace officer in my family. My grandfather was the sheriff of the county."

Alex turned to Derek. "Is your meeting over?"

"Yes. Why don't we get something to eat before we start back? Maybe on a full stomach I won't fall asleep."

Alex set her can of soda on the desk, stood and smiled at Nick. Why was it the doc managed to smile and be charming with everyone but him? Derek wondered. No—he'd take that back. She hadn't smiled or charmed Dr. Shelly. Far from it. So he was in the same class as that overinflated toad. That was a comfort, he thought sourly.

"Goodbye, ma'am. It was a real pleasure meeting you," Nick said, escorting Alex to the door.

"I enjoyed talking with you, Nick."

After they stepped outside, Derek pointed across the street. "There's the diner. It's nothing fancy, but it should meet our needs."

As Alex trailed behind Derek, the nippy, dry night air washed over her. She stopped, closed her eyes and enjoyed the glorious feeling.

"Are you all right?"

Her eyes snapped open. The darkness hid the tide of red rushing into her cheeks. "Yes. I was appreciating the dry."

"The dry?"

"The lack of humidity and the clean smell of the air. In Houston the humidity is always high and the pollution . . . let's just say this is heaven-sent."

"If you don't like Houston, why stay?"

It was the question Alex had been asking herself over and over this past month. But the problem wasn't Houston. The problem was her—Alexandra Courtland. "My job's there."

"Doc, you could get a job anywhere."

She opened her mouth to respond, but Derek had turned and walked across the street. The sign over the diner door proclaimed it to be the Blue Moon Café. It was a throwback to another time, probably the early forties, and the pink paint on the metal oval structure was peeling. The large windows allowed Alex to see the entire diner and the one waitress and three customers inside.

Derek opened the door and waited for her to precede him. Alex realized she hadn't had so many doors opened for her since she'd left Midland fifteen years earlier. Of course, old-fashioned manners were still practiced in this part of Texas. In a way it was comforting that some part of this big land remained unchanged.

Several customers called out greetings to Derek and he answered them back before he and Alex slid into a corner booth. Immediately a waitress appeared at the table, two mugs in one hand and a steaming pot of the most heavenly-smelling coffee in the other.

"Hi, Derek." The woman's smile held more than just a normal I'm-your-friendly-waitress message. Alex shook her head. Why would she care that there might be something between the deputy and this woman? "It's been a while since I've seen you."

"Lynn, how's your mother doing these days?"

"Her cancer is in remission." The young woman, maybe in her late twenties, had long black hair and dark brown eyes. Eyes that studied Alex intently.

Introductions were made and dinner ordered. After Lynn departed, Alex reached for her mug and took a swallow. "Mmm, that's good. I shouldn't be drinking coffee this late, but—" She shrugged.

Derek grinned. "Blue Moon serves the best coffee in town." He fingered the handle of the mug in front of him. "I'm sorry about the unscheduled meeting with Wes."

"Don't worry about it. Nick kept me occupied."

"I don't doubt that. Nick has a certain schoolboy charm, but don't let that fool you. He's got a sharp mind and is a good cop. It's in his blood."

Lynn reappeared with their hamburgers and fries. Before she left, she smiled again at Derek. The action irritated Alex. Biting into her burger, Alex found herself wondering about Derek's past love life. He had a daughter, but where was the child's mother? He didn't wear a wedding ring, but that didn't mean much these days.

"Are you married, Derek?" Alex could've bitten her tongue the moment the question was out of her mouth. She hadn't meant to voice the thought, but somehow it slipped out.

Derek put down his coffee mug. "I'm divorced." The words were said with such ringing finality that Alex knew the subject was closed—permanently.

Alex could well identify with his desire to keep his life private and not reveal his past. And if his ex-wife was off-limits, Alex would respect his wishes. But that didn't stop her from wondering what the ex-Mrs. Grey had done that brought such a harsh expression to Derek's eyes.

Derek rolled his shoulders to ease the tension of the long drive. Anchoring the steering wheel with his right hand, he rolled his left hand to glance at his watch. The illuminated hands indicated it was ten-fifteen.

He liked this inexpensive and uncomplicated time-piece. His ex-wife had given him a fancy digital job with alarms and whistles and more functions than a computer. He'd never worn the darn thing, didn't even want to be in the same room with it. That gift had signaled the beginning of the end of their marriage. Rhea knew he wasn't one of those guys who loved new gadgets and the latest computer games. She knew that, yet she had bought him that stupid watch.

Alexandra had fallen asleep shortly after they had begun the return trip to Saddle. Now she shifted in her sleep and murmured. Derek glanced at her. In the glow from the dash light, she looked as young and inno-cent as a sixteen-year-old. Her ponytail had come loose and her hair covered her cheek and neck. He fought the crazy urge to brush back the golden locks from her smooth cheek, and his grip on the steering wheel hardened. He had no business touching her, no business even thinking about it.

The moment of lust was a welcome break from the worry that had consumed him for the past few hours. What would he do if his little girl had TB? She seemed perfectly well at this moment, and he comforted himself with that knowledge.

Derek smiled when he thought of Sarah. She'd been the only good thing to come out of his marriage. From the instant of her birth twelve years ago, she had become the center of his world. But these past two years, since the divorce, he and Sarah had become buddies. He was still the father, and strict with his rules, but the relationship had broadened from parent-child to friends who spent nights playing Scrabble and gin rummy and eating popcorn. When he'd been a cop in San Antonio, the demands of the job had taken precious time away from his family, and he'd never had time just for play.

Derek's smile broadened as he remembered the first time Sarah had trounced him in rummy. She'd gloated for days.

Alex moaned, bringing him back to the present. Her head moved from side to side.

"Alex."

She didn't respond but continued to thrash her head. "Alexandra." He touched her arm.

"No," she shrieked, jerking awake.

Derek pulled the Jeep to the side of the road and stopped. "Alex, what's wrong?"

Her wide eyes were filled with fright, and her chest rose and fell as if she'd run for miles. She took several deep breaths and appeared calmer. But her fingers shook as she brushed back her hair, tucking the errant strands behind her ear.

"Are you all right?" Derek asked again.

She swallowed. "Fine. I just had a bad dream." One slender shoulder rose and fell. "It's nothing."

The way she held her body, her hands clutched in her lap, her shoulders hunched, head down, belied her story.

"You sure?"

She gave him an overly bright smile. "Yes."

Something was wrong, yet she wasn't admitting it. Well, it wasn't his problem.

Once they were back on the road, Alex reached out and turned on the radio. Static poured from the speakers.

"What stations do you get out here?"

"Nothing on the FM at night. Try AM."

She flipped the switch and located a station out of San Antonio, but she didn't care for the sports talk. The radio picked up several other stations from around the state, but it was more of the same. Alex didn't want to hear basketball discussed, and turned off the radio.

The darkness and silence pressed in on them. Alex leaned against the door and looked up into the night sky. "It's so beautiful out here. In the city you forget how glorious the night sky is."

"Do you like city life?" He regretted the question the instant it was out of his mouth. It made him sound nosy like Billy.

She sighed and settled back into the seat. "I never really thought about it. I went to medical school in Dallas, did work at Galveston, then went to work at the hospital in Houston. I liked the work. I never thought about the city."

"Do you ever miss Midland?"

She gave him a startled look.

"This morning you told Billy you were from there," he explained.

"Oh, yes. The conversation you overheard." Her index finger moved back and forth over her lips as she considered her answer. "Yes and no."

"A decisive answer if I've ever heard one."

She laughed. "It's hard to separate the place from the memories."

He couldn't help but ask, "Bad memories?"

"Uh . . . not really."

His brow shot up.

"My dad is a wonderful man. But he is a very forceful personality. Most of the time, he and I didn't agree on things and argued. Don't get me wrong, I love and adore him. It's just that I can't live in the same city with him. And to me, Midland and he are synonymous."

Now she'd really piqued his interest. "Who's your father?"

She hesitated. "George Anderson."

The information slammed into him like a Mack truck. "George Anderson," he muttered. Billy had really bought them trouble. George Anderson, legendary oilman and maverick, had the reputation for being a hard-nosed businessman who didn't tolerate dishonesty. Not too many men went into a fight with George and came out the winner. And if Alexandra decided to fry their bacon, she didn't have to report them to the state attorney general. All she had to do was tell her father and it would all be over.

"A bit overwhelming," she added, a twinkle in her eye. "Isn't it?"

"He's a formidable opponent," Derek answered diplomatically.

She touched his arm. "I fight my own battles, Derek. I don't ever let my dad do it for me."

He didn't doubt it. She had a sturdiness of character that came from conquering her own foes.

"But," she cautioned, "I will need to call my sister J.D. in Dallas and let her know I've been delayed. If I don't, my father will start calling folks, from the governor on down, to send out search parties for me."

That's just what Derek needed, every police agency in the state coming to Saddle and inquiring why Alex had been hijacked under his watch. "By all means, first thing you do when we get back to town is call."

She turned to look out the window, but he caught the grin curving her lips. Alex might fight her own battles, but he had the sneaking suspicion that she enjoyed people's reaction to her impressive parent.

And something told him that this apple hadn't fallen far from the tree.

Chapter 4

It had to be the cop in him. The little niggling doubt flitted around in his brain. Something didn't add up. "Tell me, if your father is George Anderson, why is your last name Courtland?" He glanced at her left hand. No wedding ring.

Alex's head jerked around and she stared at him. Even in the dim light of the car dash he could see the pain darkening her eyes.

"Are you always this suspicious or am I a special case?"

"I'm a cop, Doc. It's my job to catch inconsistencies."

His answer didn't mollify her. He didn't think she was going to answer him when she said, "If you'll recall, I was the one minding my own business and didn't ask to be thrust into this situation. I haven't tried to hustle anyone out of anything."

"I know," he quietly answered.

She took several deep, slow breaths. "I'm sorry. You asked a valid question. I'm a widow. My husband was a fellow med-school student. He was killed almost five years ago in a car accident on our second anniversary."

Derek felt lower than a dog's belly, bringing up an obviously painful memory for her. And although he'd needed to ask the question, the rationale brought him no satisfaction.

Maybe if he explained why he'd asked, she'd feel a little better. "In answer to your earlier question, yeah, I'm always that suspicious." He glanced at her and saw he had her attention. "I guess it's an occupational hazard for lawmen. We've been lied to countless times, by countless people. When you're used to seeing the bad, your brain automatically comes up with the worst-case scenario."

"I can understand that." Her words were touched with infinite sadness, and Derek felt her understanding had come from firsthand experience.

The lights of Saddle appeared as they topped the hill. "I'll need to stop and pick up Sarah. Then we can go on to my house."

"Your house? You mean you expect me to stay with you?"

"It's the only logical place, since I have a spare bedroom."

"Couldn't I stay with Mabel?"

"Sure, but you'd have to sleep on her love seat. And I doubt you'd be able to sleep past five when she gets up. She lives above her restaurant, and I've heard she makes a real racket in her kitchen. Roosters take their cue from her."

"Isn't there somewhere else I could stay?"

Her attitude was quickly becoming annoying. She was acting as if he was going to try to seduce her. He had a daughter, for Pete's sakes. Did she think he was going to chase her around with Sarah in the house? Never mind that the good doc did a number on his libido and that he found her more attractive than he'd found any other woman for a long, long time.

"You could try to stay at Doc Talbot's old place."

"That sounds fine," she responded a little too quickly.

"'Course, I can't guarantee that anything in the house will work. Or for that matter, I have no idea what the inside of the house looks like. The place has been closed up for nearly a year and a half."

"Oh."

"We can try it if you like. But I got to warn you. Although it's May, the nights around here get cool. You might need a heater."

She sighed. "I don't want to make more work for you than necessary. Thanks for the offer."

Odd, she didn't sound thankful. Well, come to think of it, neither was he.

The first glimpse Alex had of Sarah was when she stumbled out Mabel's front door. The twelve-year-old was tall for her age, with long, golden hair that whipped around her face as she walked to the car. Derek opened the back door for his daughter and in the harsh overhead light, Sarah looked pale and tired. It was past midnight, Alex argued to herself, and the girl had probably been sleeping.

"Hello," Sarah said shyly.

Alex felt a tiny edge of her frozen heart soften. "Hi, Sarah. I'm Alex."

"I know." The girl's eyes were deep brown, just like her father's.

Derek slid behind the steering wheel. "Our house is on the next street."

"It's not hard to find," Sarah said, an odd note in her voice, "since there are only three streets in this town."

Alex looked over her shoulder. "Then I guess it's hard to get lost in Saddle."

"Yeah."

"At least there's no traffic," Derek said, pulling into the driveway of his house.

"You're lucky," Alex replied, getting out of the Jeep. "My drive from the hospital in Houston to my town house should only take ten minutes. It rarely does."

Alex felt Derek's unvoiced question again asking why she stayed. Once inside the house, Sarah turned to her father. "Is Alex going to stay here with us?"

In the warm light cast by the living-room lamps Alex could see what a beautiful woman Sarah would one day become. "Your father has graciously offered me your spare bedroom until my car is fixed. I hope you don't mind."

The girl brightened. "No. I think it will be nice to have you here. Dad, you want me to show Alex to the guest room?"

"I'll do that, sweetheart," Derek answered. "Why don't you go on to bed. You have school tomorrow."

Alex saw the disappointment in Sarah's eyes before she quickly hid it. "All right. I'll see you tomorrow." She kissed her father on the cheek, smiled at Alex and disappeared down the hall.

"Would you like a cup of coffee before turning in?"

Alex sensed there was more to the offer than just a nightcap. "Sure."

She followed him into the small kitchen, noting that the white countertops and appliances were a marked contrast to the dark wood cabinets. Derek grabbed the shiny teakettle from the stove and filled it with water.

"Do you have decaf?" she asked.

He gave her a horrified look. "That's like buying an impotent bull. Why have him?"

A chuckle bubbled up her throat and although she tried to suppress the sound, it escaped. It was odd, Alex thought, to hear her own laughter after so long a time without it.

He grinned in response and his reaction sent a jolt of awareness down Alex's spine. Here she was, alone with this man, in the middle of the night, in his house, five hundred miles from her little condo. This was no time for her body to start having lustful impulses.

"So I take it you don't have decaf?"

"You got it. But the offer for real coffee is still open." His mouth curved into a sexy grin.

"If I have a jolt of caffeine this late, I'll be awake all night. I was pushing it with that cup at the Blue Moon. Would you happen to have some herbal tea?"

His expression was priceless. "Doc, I'm a cop. I drink hundred-proof, unadulterated coffee, period."

He struck her as that type—an alpha male. The poor man wouldn't be caught dead drinking herbal tea. He probably also ate fried foods, liked red meat and had real butter on his bread. She would love to do a cholesterol screen on him. "What does Sarah drink?"

He leaned his hip against the countertop and folded his arms across his wide chest. More of those little sparks of awareness danced over Alex's skin.

"Sarah drinks milk and soft drinks. You're welcome to either one." He motioned toward the refrigerator. "Take a look inside and see if anything appeals to you."

Alex had no intention of searching through his refrigerator. Somehow it seemed too intimate an activity. "How about some hot milk?"

He didn't say anything for a moment. "Are you sure?" From his tone it was apparent he thought she'd taken leave of her senses.

"I'm sure."

He shrugged and pulled a pan from the drawer at the bottom of the stove. As she watched him pour the milk, Alex remembered the call she needed to make.

"Would you mind if I used your phone to call my sister?"

He glanced at his watch. "It's after midnight. You sure you don't want to wait until morning?"

"I'm sure. J.D. was expecting me to call tonight after I got home. She'll be worried. Also, we'll all sleep better knowing my father won't have reason to be concerned."

"Why not call him?"

Apparently the deputy hadn't had to deal with her father in person. "Derek, you've never met my dad, have you?"

He shook his head.

It was hard to explain her relationship with her father. "Well, let's just say I want to sleep after the call. If I talk to him, I'll spend the night worrying that he'll show up here in the morning, wanting to know what's

going on.'' She gave him a smile. ''I don't think either of us wants that, do we?''

''You've got a point.''

''I know.'' She picked up the receiver on the wall
phone in the kitchen and dialed her sister's number in
Dallas.

''Hello,'' a sleepy male voice answered.

''Luke, this is Alex. Can I talk to J.D.?''

''Are you all right, Alex?'' Luke's voice became
clear and pointed.

''I'm fine.''

After a moment of silence J.D. came on the line.
''Alex, are you okay? What happened? I've been
worried sick about your safety. You should've been
home a couple of hours ago.''

Alex bit back the desire to laugh. Her sister was a
force to be reckoned with, more than an equal match
for their father. ''I'm sorry I didn't call sooner, sis. I
had car trouble.''

''Where are you?''

Alex glanced at Derek. ''I'm in a little town called
Saddle in Brewster County. The water pump on my car
went out. It's going to take several days to get it
fixed.''

''You need someone to come get you?''

''No. I just wanted to let you know where I was.
Also, if Dad calls and asks you where I am, you can
tell him.''

''Okay. Is there anything else? Are you sure you're
all right?''

Leave it to her sister to pick up the note of exasperation in her voice. ''Everything is just fine, sis. The
deputy sheriff and his daughter have offered me a
room while I'm here.''

In the pause that followed, Alex knew her sister was stewing over the tone of her voice. Alex just prayed J.D. would let the matter go. "Give me the number where I can reach you?"

Alex put her hand over the mouthpiece. "What's your phone number?" she asked Derek.

He gave her the number and she repeated it into the phone.

"If you need anything," J.D. said, "call me."

Alex breathed a sigh of relief. "I will. Give that baby of yours a kiss for me." She hung up and turned to Derek.

"Is your sister as bad as your dad?"

A laugh burst from her lips. "How'd you know?"

"Your face showed it."

He stood by the table, the mugs of coffee and milk before him, and held out a chair for her. After all this time, it was odd to have a male show such chivalry. It felt good. He seated her, then sat beside her.

They drank their hot drinks for several moments before he spoke. "What do you think about Sarah?"

"What do you mean? Do you mean do I think she's a beautiful young woman? Yes, I do. Or are you asking about her health?"

"Do you think she's sick?" The tone of his voice and the expression on his face told Alex this man cared deeply for his child.

"It's impossible to say at this point. First we need to establish if Norma has TB. Has Sarah been sick?"

Derek rubbed his forehead, than ran his fingers through his hair. "She had the flu this winter and a couple of colds, but nothing out of the ordinary."

"What about this last month? Has she had any complaints?"

"No. She's appeared just fine."

"Then let's wait on Norma's test results before we worry."

His broad shoulders relaxed. "Drink up, Doc. Six-thirty rolls around mighty quick, and you're looking like you need a good night's sleep."

"You're not looking so great yourself, Deputy." But even as she said it, Alex knew that in spite of his haggard appearance, he was a fine-looking man.

He laughed. "A guy sure isn't going to get a swelled head around you, is he?"

"I call 'em as I see 'em."

"Ouch," he said with a pained expression. "C'mon, I'll show you to your room."

Derek put their mugs in the sink and walked into the living room. He picked up her leather bag and led the way down the hall, pointing out the bathroom and then her room. "It's not fancy," he explained as he opened the door and flipped on the light, "but the mattress is a good one."

She stepped into the room and looked around. The blond bedroom set had simple lines and a white chenille bedspread covered the double bed. There were no little knickknacks, plants or pictures on the dresser or nightstand. But despite the barrenness, Alex appreciated having a real bed. Anything was better than Bosnia.

"This is fine. Thank you." She turned and found herself nose-to-nose, or really nose-to-chest, with him. Suddenly it was hard to catch her breath. His warm, hard chest filled her field of vision. The top button of his shirt was open and Alex fought a sudden urge to touch the tanned, smooth skin of his chest. Why could a uniform make a man look so masculine?

Unconsciously her tongue darted out to moisten her dry lips. Slowly she tipped her head back to say goodnight but the words died in her throat when her gaze collided with his. His brown eyes had turned nearly black with heat.

For what seemed an eternity they were caught in an erotic web where every sense came painfully and gloriously alive. Alex's mind was swamped with images of this man, of touching him, of loving him.

Fear and caution cut through the clingy tendrils of sensuality, bringing her back to reality. "Good night." The words were a mere whisper, but they were all she could do at the moment.

Once behind the safety of the closed door, Alex leaned against the solid strength of the wood. What was wrong with her to be fantasizing about Derek like that? Had she really gone off her rocker? She walked to the bed and sank onto its softness, stretched out without taking her shoes off and pulled a pillow to her chest.

What was happening to her? After her husband had been killed, Alex had never really dealt with the pain but instead buried herself in the practice of medicine. There had been no "Alex" outside her job. When she had volunteered to go to Bosnia with the Red Cross, she'd wanted to give to those hurting people. But there had been too many she couldn't save, and too many she couldn't help. She had tried to ignore the emotional pain as she'd done before, only this time it didn't work. Medicine was no longer her refuge, as she had discovered when she'd stepped back into the emergency room. This past month she had felt as if her heart had been frozen, because all her emotions seemed cold and colorless.

So why all of a sudden was she behaving like a giddy, pubescent girl?

Alex clutched the pillow harder and pressed her face into the softness, fighting the tears that threatened, because she knew if she started to cry, she wouldn't stop.

The sound of running water woke Alex the next morning. Her eyes fluttered open and she tried to remember where she was. Derek Grey's house in Saddle, Texas. Rolling onto her back, she moaned at the crick in her neck and realized she'd fallen asleep in her clothes and shoes. Her mouth tasted as if it was coated with a thick layer of west Texas dust.

The water shut off, leaving her room quiet.

With care Alex sat up and spied her suitcase sitting beside the door where Derek had left it last night. Retrieving fresh clothes and her toothbrush, Alex hurried to the bathroom. As she reached the door, it opened inward and Derek stood there, bare to the waist and freshly shaved.

The shock and sensual thrill that raced through Alex caused her jaw to go slack. Derek's eyes danced in amusement as he surveyed her from her disheveled hair to the bottom of the running shoes she'd had on for the past twenty-four hours.

His mouth curved into a devastating smile. "How did you sleep?" he asked.

Alex's brain was only operating on forty-percent capacity, and she wasn't up to witty repartee at this time of the morning. Still, he'd asked a civil question.

"Fine," she mumbled, keeping her head down for fear of breathing in his face. Her gaze swept over the sculptured planes of his chest. It was tanned, smooth, with the muscles of his abdomen well defined. When she realized that she was staring, she jerked her gaze to his face.

"Are you one of those persons who needs coffee in the morning before they can talk?" He sounded as if he was enjoying himself.

She really didn't need this. It would be easier to deal with Derek's masculine appeal after she had a shower and brushed her teeth. She motioned to the bathroom behind him. "Are you finished?" she asked through stiff lips.

"Yes." He stepped aside. "By the time you're done, Sarah and I should have breakfast ready."

She nodded, then slipped past him and closed the door behind her.

For Derek, it had been quite a shock to open the bathroom door and find the good doctor standing there. With her mussed hair and sleepy-eyed look, she was like a dream come true. Luckily, when she opened her mouth, the image evaporated and her grumpy disposition became evident. At that point, the temptation to tease her had overwhelmed him.

As Derek pulled a clean uniform shirt from his closet he warned himself not to get involved with this woman. She was here temporarily, until her car was fixed. Besides, he wasn't looking for another long-term relationship with a woman, not after the ugly divorce he'd been through.

When he entered the kitchen, Sarah had the pancake batter ready.

"Good morning," Sarah greeted him cheerfully. "Is Alex up?"

"She's getting ready in the bathroom. She should be here in a few minutes."

"Oh." Sarah poured the orange juice into the glasses and sat down. "I think she's real pretty."

Derek paused with a ladle of batter poised over the hot skillet. "Who?"

Sarah gave him an exasperated sigh. "Dr. Alex. Don't you think she's pretty?"

"I suppose," he muttered as he finished pouring batter.

"Really, Dad."

"Why don't you get the butter and syrup," he said, trying to get her off the subject of his fantasies.

"Sure."

By the time he'd finished fixing the second stack of pancakes, Alex showed up.

"Good morning," she greeted everyone in a much more approachable voice than she'd used with him earlier. "Am I too late to be fed?" Her stomach rumbled and she blushed.

"Nope," Derek replied. "Take this stack of pancakes and I'll make another."

"Thanks."

Alex sat next to Sarah. "I'll bet these pancakes are as good as they smell." As Alex buttered her stack, she glanced at Sarah several times but said nothing. After she took a bite, she moaned in delight. "These are wonderful, Derek."

"The credit belongs to Sarah. She made the batter from scratch."

"My compliments, Sarah. Personally, all I can cook is microwave stuff."

The girl laughed. "Yeah, that's Dad's specialty, too."

Alex took another bite and the flavor of banana melted in her mouth. "Banana pancakes?"

Sarah nodded.

"I never would've thought to put bananas in pancake batter."

"That was Sarah's idea," Derek offered, pride ringing in his voice. "She came up with the idea one morning when we ran out of blueberries. My daughter is one smart girl."

Sarah glowed under her father's praise, and it was obvious that the deputy loved her.

The breakfast conversation passed pleasantly. As they lingered over juice and coffee, the telephone rang. Derek answered it.

"Good morning, Norma. Yeah, the doctor's here. You want to speak to her?" Derek held out the receiver to Alex.

Alex took the white handpiece and lifted it to her ear. Norma's call had brought back into focus the crisis the town might be facing. "How are you feeling this morning, Norma?"

"I had a bad night, Doc. I was wondering if you got the test yesterday?"

"Yes, Deputy Grey and I did. Why don't I meet you at the clinic in five minutes? Can you do that?"

"I can. I'll see you there."

The instant she hung up, Derek asked, "Would you like for me to drive you?"

"No. I'll walk. Breakfast was wonderful."

As Alex walked to the clinic she prayed that this time she'd missed the diagnosis and it wasn't TB.

Derek drove his Jeep the one block from his house to the sheriff's office. As he parked the vehicle, he saw the school bus waiting in front of the feed store.

"You better hurry," Derek told his daughter.

Sarah grabbed her backpack and started to open the door.

"Don't I get a kiss?" he asked.

Sarah leaned over and brushed a kiss across his cheek. "Bye." She slammed the door and hurried toward the bus.

After waving goodbye, Derek walked down the street to the clinic. Inside, he found Alex sitting behind Doc Talbot's desk. From the way she was slumped in the chair, he knew she was worried.

"Have you finished your test on Norma?" he asked, coming into the room.

The weight of the world seemed to rest on her slender shoulders. "Yes."

"And you're still convinced she has TB?"

She didn't answer verbally, but what she felt was reflected in her eyes.

"Is that why you look so down in the mouth?"

"I look that bad?"

"C'mon, Doc. You're a beautiful woman, but you got that look that says you're not happy."

"And since when are you an expert on a woman's expression?"

"That one I know well. My ex-wife flashed me that look so many times, I know all its shades. Now, what are you not telling me?"

She pursed her lips and moved them from side to side, then heaved a sigh. "Norma's very upset. She's afraid she's infected everyone in town."

"And I suppose you told her not to borrow trouble."

Alex's eyes went wide.

"It's your trademark line."

She stood. "Well, it's true. Tomorrow has enough trouble of its own. We need to deal with today's." She started toward the door.

"Where you going?"

Her footsteps halted. She didn't look back at him. "I don't know. Maybe I can find a good book over at the feed store."

Laughter rumbled in Derek's chest. "All you're going to find at Fred's store is a copy of a hardware catalog and the latest edition of *Cattle and Feed* magazine."

She whirled. "Do you have a better suggestion on how to while away my day? There aren't a lot of options open to me." Her blue eyes turned an intriguing color of indigo when she was mad.

"Yeah, I do. I thought you might like to go out to my ranch and spend some time. I know I promised you that yesterday."

"I thought you said it was your family's ranch."

"It is. My younger brother and I are fifty-fifty owners. Because of my job with the sheriff's department, Todd runs the ranch and takes care of things. So, are you game, or do you want to try the feed store?"

She leaned against the doorframe. "Are you going to let me go horseback riding?"

"Sure." He walked toward her. "I'll even let you chase cattle if you want."

"I'll pass on the steer chasing, but I'll hold you to the promise of a ride."

Derek settled his Stetson on his head. "Anything your heart desires, Doc. You got it."

"What I want, Deputy, is my car repaired."

"Sorry, ma'am, that's one miracle that's out of my control. But anything else you want, just let me know."

She gave him a speculative look that gave him a chill up his spine. He just might have opened himself up to more trouble than he could handle.

Chapter 5

The first sight of the sprawling stone ranch house brought a painful little twist to Alex's heart. As Derek's Jeep sped over the unpaved road Alex wondered why her heart reacted in such a manner. This area of west Texas didn't resemble Midland. Here there were mountains and hills, whereas the place she'd grown up was endless flatlands. So why did this place feel familiar, as if she was coming home after a long absence?

Fatigue, she told herself. She was tired, that's all.

"My great-grandfather built the original structure some hundred and twenty years ago. Since then, each generation has added something to it, if only electricity and running water."

"Those are big improvements," she said with heartfelt earnestness, having lived without such basic benefits for a prolonged time this past year.

He laughed. "You can't tell me your daddy doesn't have those amenities in his house."

"You're right, but I haven't lived with my father for a long time."

Derek's gaze traveled over her face and Alex felt the heat and interest in his eyes. "You make it sound as if you're ancient. From what I can see, you're in the prime of your life."

She wished she felt in her prime, but inside she felt old and tired. "Looks can be deceiving."

He frowned and Alex turned away from his penetrating stare.

"I don't know if anyone will see us coming," Derek said as he turned the Jeep onto the pebbled driveway. "I tried calling before we left, but I didn't get anyone. My brother and his wife are probably off working somewhere on the ranch."

He stopped the Jeep before the front door. "Anyone home?" he called as he got out and walked around the front of the vehicle. "Cathy, Todd, you here?"

Derek opened the passenger door and helped Alex out.

A tall man emerged from a side building Alex guessed to be the barn. At the same time a petite woman opened the front door.

"Derek, what are you doing here, yelling your head off?" asked the man striding toward them. The closer he got, the more obvious it became that he was Derek's brother. As tall as Derek, he had brown hair a little darker than his brother's, but his grin was just as sexy as the deputy's.

Ignoring Todd, Derek turned to the woman, giving her a big hug. "Hello, Cathy, you're looking as pretty as ever."

The young woman smiled, her eyes lighting with delight. "Thanks, you silver-tongued devil."

Todd joined his wife. Derek grabbed Alex's hand, brought her to his side and made the introductions.

After exchanging pleasantries, Todd asked, "So what are you doing out here in the middle of the week?"

Cathy elbowed her husband. "Mind your manners, Todd Grey. Ask them inside for coffee before you start grilling them."

Todd shrugged.

"Alex, would you like a cup of coffee and a slice of some bread fresh out of the oven?" Cathy asked, ignoring both of the men.

"That sounds wonderful."

"Good." Cathy motioned for Alex to go with her. The men exchanged a look and followed.

The inside of the house was a cozy mixture of well-worn leather furniture and carefully cared-for antique wooden pieces. A Remington bronze of a cowboy on his horse sat on a side table. Warm colors and Western art decorated the living room. In front of the massive stone fireplace was a braided rag rug. An image of Derek and Todd as children popped into Alex's head, and she could almost hear them laughing and running through this house. As she walked along, she wondered if Derek had any other brothers or sisters.

The bright, modern kitchen was filled with the mouth-watering aroma of freshly baked bread. Todd poured coffee into mugs while Cathy cut slices of the bread.

When Todd placed a mug in front of Alex, Derek asked, "You sure you want coffee? I thought caffeine bothered you."

"She doesn't like coffee?" Cathy asked. "I've got regular tea and even some herbal tea."

Last night's conversation with Derek came to mind. Alex glanced at him and saw he was remembering it, too. Apparently Derek's sister-in-law had more diverse tastes than he did. "Coffee is fine."

"Are you sure?" Cathy asked. "Making you some tea would be no problem."

"I'm sure."

After everyone was seated, Todd repeated his earlier question. "So, why are you here?"

"A couple of reasons," Derek answered. "First, I came out to talk to you about what I learned last night from the sheriff. DEA thinks there's a smuggling ring operating in this part of the county. They've spotted a low-flying plane entering and leaving this area, but they lose the plane right around Split-Tree Rock." He took a sip of his coffee.

"What? You mean someone is smuggling drugs close to our ranch?"

"At this point, we don't know," Derek answered. "The DEA wants to use the ranch as a base of operations to search for a landing strip. I told Wes that I had to check with you two since you are the ones who would have to put up with the agents. Do you have any objections?"

"Damn," Todd said, rubbing his forehead. "I knew something was wrong."

"What are you talking about?" Derek demanded.

"During the past month I've heard a plane a couple of times late at night. Once, the noise woke me up.

I told myself that it was nothing. You know how sound travels out here. I convinced myself it was air traffic going into El Paso. But I should've known better, as crazy as the world is these days."

"Why didn't you mention it to me? You know, Todd, that *is* part of my job."

The younger man shrugged. "I guess I just didn't want it to be true. I keep hoping that things will be like they were when we were kids."

Alex saw regret at the passing of a simpler time on the faces gathered around the table. She could share their sadness. Somehow in the past few years it seemed as if everyone had gone crazy and there were no sane folks left in this world.

"Is it all right if the DEA guys set up shop here?" Derek turned to Cathy. "Can you put up with them roaming through your house? They're on their way right now, but I can send them back if it's a problem."

"It's fine," Cathy replied. "Anything we can do to help, we'll do."

Todd's expression darkened. "Do you think any of our neighbors are involved with this smuggling?"

The ugly prospect hung like a pall in the room. "I can't say for sure that this is a smuggling case."

"Then why's someone flying into this part of the county?" Todd asked.

There was no reasonable explanation except smuggling activity. Derek lifted his mug to his lips and found it dry. "Could I have a refill?"

Todd retrieved the coffeepot and poured Derek more coffee. "You said there were two reasons you came out here today. What's the second?"

"Alexandra. She's stuck in Saddle for a couple of days and I thought she would enjoy spending some of her time out here. There's not a lot to do in town, if you're not a rancher or picking up your mail."

At the mention of mail, Alex wondered if Derek would tell his brother about the possibility of Norma having TB. Alex hoped he wouldn't. She didn't see the point of worrying anyone needlessly until they got the test results.

"You going to have her out checking steers?" Todd questioned, his tone dry. "Or better yet, the vet from Marfa hasn't been here this week. Maybe I could consult with her about that sick cow I have."

Derek's eyes narrowed. "I brought her out here, little brother, so she wouldn't have to doctor everyone in town."

Alex couldn't help grinning. "I limit my practice to patients with two legs. And if they have a tail, well, that's definitely out of my league."

Before the brothers could exchange any more quips, they heard a car drive up out front. Derek stood and walked to the window.

"It looks like the DEA guys are here." Derek turned to Alex. "As soon as I'm done with these guys, I promise we'll go out riding."

"I'll be here."

Oddly enough, she was looking forward to riding with him. The question that worried her was why?

The familiar smells of the barn—the hay, the warm horseflesh, the manure—reached across the years and touched Alex's soul with warmth. When she was growing up, her father had kept horses for her and her sisters to ride. Alex had loved her quarter horse and they had won several ribbons in cutting competition. Once she'd gone away to college, then medical school, there had never been any time for this passion. It had fallen by the wayside, like so many other things in her life. After her youngest sister's accident, medicine had been the end-all and be-all of Alex's life.

A meow of a cat caught her attention. "Here, kitty," she called softly. "Here, kitty, kitty."

Searching the soft shadows of the barn, Alex tried to find the source of the meowing.

She was drawn to an empty stall. A large tabby cat was curled in the clean hay. "Hello," she said, walking into the stall. "You're a fat, contented fellow, aren't you?"

"That he is." Derek's voice came from behind her. "Charlie, there, is one spoiled cat."

She turned to him. "Is everything worked out with the DEA agents?"

"Yeah, they're setting up." From his tone and manner, Alex wondered what problems had occurred. He seemed to shake himself out of his dark thoughts and smiled at her. That smile of his always managed to make her heart skip a beat. "You ready for that ride?"

"Yes."

Derek picked out two mounts and saddled them. Together he and Alex rode west into the rising hills. The tall mountains in the distance were beautiful, white peaks against the deep blue sky.

"As kids, Todd and I rode through these hills, learning every inch of the ranch. We used to pretend we were the first white men to see this land, just like our great-grandfathers." He stopped his horse and looked down at the valley below. "Those were hardy men and women who settled these parts. Sometimes I wonder how they did it.''

Alex watched the play of emotions on Derek's face. It was obvious that he loved the land and was proud of the life his parents and grandparents had carved out. She looked out over the vista, trying to see it through his eyes, trying to understand his love for the place. For Alex, when she was growing up, all she had wanted to do was leave west Texas behind, with its heat and sandstorms and hardness. Of course, Midland was miles and miles of flatlands, whereas in this area of west Texas, volcanic and limestone mountains were part of the landscape.

''What brought your family to this part of Texas?'' she asked.

''Nick's great-grandfather and mine came with the army. After they mustered out, they both stayed and started their dynasties.''

Alex had friends in Midland whose grandparents had settled the land. Each successive generation had lived in the same spot, never leaving the county. The only exceptions were the soldiers drafted for war.

''Have you ever been outside Brewster County?'' Once voiced, her question sounded rude even to her own ears.

She watched in amazement as his body tensed and his expression changed from relaxed to harsh. He pierced her with a laser-sharp look. ''Yeah, I've been outside the county. Let's see, I saw Beirut, Grenada, El Salvador.''

Those places rang a bell in her mind. They were all trouble spots.

"Ah, I see you recognize names where the U.S. military has been." The sarcasm in his voice made her wince inwardly.

She certainly had hit a sensitive spot. "You were in the military." An obvious conclusion.

He gave her a curt nod. "I served in the marines for eight years. Afterward, I joined the San Antonio police force and was a cop for another nine years."

She felt like an idiot. She argued with herself that she hadn't meant to insult him, had only wanted to learn more about him. And she had, but she'd hurt him in the process. And still she didn't have a clue as to what he saw in these barren hills.

Derek nudged his horse forward and started down from the hilltop. Watching his rigid spine as he rode away, Alex knew she had to apologize. She rode after him.

"Derek," she called. He slowed his mount. Once she was beside him she looked him directly in the eye. "I need to apologize. I didn't mean to be rude."

His expression didn't change, but at least he was listening. That gave her a ray of hope.

"My question kind of came out sideways."

A muscle in his cheek twitched, and she thought he might be trying to suppress a smile. "Sideways?"

She lifted her shoulder and gave him a sheepish look. "It came out harsher than I meant it. You see, growing up in Midland, all I wanted to do was escape. Go somewhere where trees grew in abundance and there was a shape to the landscape other than flat. Of course, my view might be colored by my feelings for my dad."

He cocked his head. "What does your dad have to do with anything?"

"Everything." How could she explain about her father? How did one express the tangled feelings that she and her two sisters had for their dad? It was like trying to explain the jet stream. Maybe if she told Derek about her car, that would show him. "You want to know why I drive a '66 Mustang?"

"What's a car got to do with Midland or, for that matter, your dad?"

"I bought that car when I turned sixteen. With my own money. Money I earned myself. It was old and needed repairs, but that didn't matter since it was all I could afford. My dad told me to take it back, that he could afford to buy his daughter a brand-new Mustang."

The horses reached the floor of the valley and were pulled to a stop. Derek dismounted and checked his horse's right front hoof. He brought his knife out of the front pocket of his pants and dislodged a stone.

"Is he okay?" Alex asked, nodding to the gray gelding.

"I caught it early enough, but just to make sure, I want to walk him a little."

Alex slid off her horse, grabbed the reins and fell into step with Derek.

"I take it you didn't accept your father's offer of a new car."

Memories of the two days of arguments and tantrums between her and her father washed over Alex in waves. "In the end, I won, but only after a lot of heated discussion."

One dark eyebrow arched and he gave her a speculative look. "Heated discussion? Is that what it's now called?"

"It is the polite terminology for a family donny-brook."

"Why did you want the old car when you could've had your father pay for a new one?"

"Because I wanted to do something on my own, something that my dad hadn't provided or arranged because of his influence. I wanted to feel . . ." *Worthy of people's respect.* That was the real reason she'd fought so hard. She had needed to be valued for who she was, not who her father was. But she didn't feel comfortable sharing that deep truth with a man she'd known less than thirty hours.

"What did you want to feel?" he softly queried.

They stopped and Alex was trapped by the deep quiet reflected in his face, as if he were sincerely interested in the emotions of a sixteen-year-old girl. And try as she might, she couldn't ignore his tenderness.

"I didn't want to be known as just one of George Anderson's girls." She stared at the reins in her hand. "I wanted to be known as Alexandra, George's strange middle child, who wanted only to be given what she earned."

"I bet that rubbed your father's pride the wrong way."

The memory of her father calling her a willful and ungrateful teenager blossomed in her brain and she laughed. "Oh, yes, and he told me about it numerous times."

"But he let you keep the car."

"Only after he bought a new Mustang and parked it in our garage. After six weeks of it sitting there, he took it back." Turning her upper body, she looked up at him. "When he came back from the dealership that day, he gave me a big hug and told me he was proud of me."

Derek stopped and patted his horse on the neck. "Did your relationship with your dad improve after that?"

"It was never sour. It was just that Dad tries to live everyone's life for them. If you don't stand up for yourself, then you find yourself doing a lot of things you don't like.

"After I bought my car, Dad resisted my ideas as strongly as he had before. The man never quits."

"And that's why you don't like west Texas?"

"It sounds stupid, I know, but my memories of my dad can't be divided from the place. That's why I wanted to know why you love this place. I wanted another view besides my own."

With his forefinger Derek pushed his Stetson back on his head. "Why do I love this place?" His horse nickered and Derek rubbed him between his eyes. "I tried for seventeen years to live a life-style that wasn't the one in my soul. I finally woke up one morning and decided to be what I was, a cowboy who's also a cop. When the job of deputy sheriff opened up, I grabbed it." His gaze ran over the horizon, then returned to her. "I haven't regretted the decision for one moment. In fact, I wish I'd gotten smart earlier before the big-city problems found their way out here." He straightened his hat. "It's getting late and I need to get back to town. You ready?"

"Yes."

As they rode back to the barn, Alex tried again to see the land through Derek's eyes. She didn't think she was successful, except for the soothing feel of the wind on her face.

After saying goodbye to his brother and sister-in-law, and watching the two DEA agents admire and laugh with Alex, Derek escorted her to his Jeep.

"They're very charming," Alex said, buckling her seat belt.

Derek paused in starting the engine. "You think those two feds are charming?"

Alex gave him a startled look. "The feds?"

Turning the key in the ignition, he kept his eyes straight ahead. "Yeah. Those DEA agents."

"No, no," she replied. "I wasn't talking about the agents. I was talking about your brother and his wife."

He glanced over his shoulder and saw the amusement in her face. Sunlight danced in red and gold highlights in her hair. Her smooth skin was the color of rich cream, her cheeks pink with health, her lips the color of strawberries. He wondered if they were as sweet. His gaze moved over her face and collided with blue eyes. Like a bolt of lightning, heat and awareness flashed between them, sizzling every nerve ending in his body.

Alex broke the contact by staring down at her hands. "I like them."

Derek's mind groped to remember what they were talking about. That was one of the things about lightning, it tended to short-circuit things.

"Todd and Cathy," she added in explanation. "I like them."

He shook off the lust-filled haze surrounding his brain, put the Jeep into gear and started down the driveway. "They're good folks. They worked this ranch and kept it alive after my dad died and while I was gone."

"I assume you didn't mention the suspected TB to them because it's not positive yet?" she asked.

"Yeah. No sense alarming them if we don't have to."

"I agree."

"On the other hand, with doctors as scarce as they are out here, we have to be prepared."

"Is this a plug for getting your own doctor in town?" She sounded as if she suspected him of taking her out to the ranch for other reasons than to go horseback riding. Glancing at her, he saw that her expression confirmed what he'd heard in her voice.

Anger flashed through him. This was not the first time she'd questioned his integrity. Earlier she'd accused him of being in cahoots with Billy Mayer to disable her car. Now she was implying that he was spending time with her for something other than the pleasure of her company.

"No." His voice rang with his irritation. "It isn't. I took you out to the ranch for the reason I said. As a matter of fact, I was concerned that maybe some of the folks around here would hear you were in town and show up at the clinic." He clenched his teeth, trying not to say anything he might regret later.

They drove in silence the rest of the way to Saddle. Derek drove by the clinic and saw a truck parked in front of the building. A young woman holding a baby was pacing back and forth before the front door. When she saw Derek, she waved him down. With a glance at Alex, Derek pulled up beside the truck. Instantly the woman rushed to the driver's side of the Jeep.

This is exactly what Derek had feared would happen. But seeing the panic on Terri Hansen's face, he couldn't worry about what Alex thought. Rolling down the window, Derek asked, "Terri, what's wrong?"

"I'm so glad you're here. I've been waiting almost a half-hour and was about to drive to Alpine. It's the baby." Fear clouded her words. "He's running a fever of a hundred and four. I can't get it to come down." A sob caught in her throat. "I was hoping..." She looked expectantly at Alex. "I heard about the doctor and thought I'd come into town to see if she could help. The drive to Alpine is so far and the baby's so sick."

Derek and Terri turned to Alex. She sat stiffly in the seat, staring at the sign on the clinic wall. Derek had the odd feeling that Alex was battling herself. Finally, after a long pause, she looked at Terri. "Come on inside, and I'll take a look at your baby."

Terri's shoulders slumped in relief. "Thank you," she choked out.

At the door of the clinic Derek stopped Alex. "You don't need me in there. I'll check in at my office to make sure everything's all right. Be back in a few minutes."

He watched the women disappear into the building, then walked to his office. As he strode down the sidewalk, he wondered what battle Alex was fighting, because sure as cactus had thorns, something bad was bothering the doc.

Alex sat down and smiled wearily at Terri. After an hour of pouring tepid water over the baby and administering a fever-reducing agent, the baby's temperature was down to one hundred.

"You'll have to keep up with the medicine, and if his temperature goes up past a hundred and one, you'll need to bathe him like we did here." Alex pushed across the desk a sample of an antibiotic. "This is all that's here at the clinic. I'll write a prescription for more."

"Thank you, Dr. Courtland. I don't know what I would've done if you weren't here. I got so scared. One minute he was fussing, then the next he was burning up with fever."

The feeling of being trapped began to close around Alex's heart. To be needed. Was it a blessing or a curse? "That happens all the time with babies. Their little bodies heat up quickly. But by the same token, they get over things much quicker than adults."

Terri took the medicine and stood. "What do I owe you?"

"Nothing."

"I want to pay you," Terri insisted.

Her car and the repairs to it came to mind. "I've already been paid, so don't worry."

Terri hesitated, then nodded and hurried out.

Alex leaned back in the big leather chair and closed her eyes. Images of another sixteen-month-old crowded in on her. That little girl had died in her arms because of the simple lack of antibiotic and the merciless soldiers who held up the medical convoy.

Grief and pain twisted her heart. Alex fought to clamp a lid on the emotions that threatened to spill out. Once that Pandora's box was opened, she didn't know what would pour out. Alexandra leaped to her feet and headed out of the clinic.

At that instant Sarah appeared at the front door. "Hi, Alex. Dad said you were down here with Terri and her baby." She glanced around. "Are they gone?"

"Yes. How was your day?"

The girl gave it a moment's thought. "Okay. I came by to ask you if you wanted to help me cook dinner tonight."

The hope shining in Sarah's eyes made it impossible to refuse. "You realize I'm a lousy cook."

The girl gave her a wide smile. "I remember. But all you'll need to do is make a salad." From the delight on her young face, Alex guessed that what Sarah wanted was company, not another chef. And that she could provide.

"Okay, Sarah, I'm yours."

Chapter 6

Derek opened the front door of his house and froze at the sound of the female voices coming from the kitchen.

"This is wonderful, Sarah." Alex's mellow voice skimmed over Derek's skin in a provocative wave, making him painfully aware that he'd been without a woman since well before his divorce.

His daughter's laughter, light and carefree, cut through the sensual fog surrounding his brain. Derek took a deep breath, trying to get his emotions under control. This was the first time in two years that he'd heard his daughter laugh with such abandon.

"It's a bottled sauce," Sarah answered.

"You have an extraordinary talent for opening the jar and heating it up."

"You're teasing me."

"I wish I was. I've burned more things on the top

of the stove than I care to think about. Why, one week I set off my smoke alarm three times.''

Sarah chuckled again and Derek leaned back against the door, enjoying the sound.

''It's the gospel truth. The fire department declared my cooktop a fire hazard and forbade me to use it again.''

Derek shook his head. Was Alex simply teasing Sarah, or was she that bad a cook? If the past day was any indication of her sense of humor, or lack of it, then she was telling Sarah the truth. So far, most of what he'd seen of the lady was her grouchy side.

''Now I know you're pulling my leg,'' Sarah answered.

Derek silently walked down the hall to the kitchen.

''Maybe a little. But the station chief came by after the last incident with a grocery bag of frozen microwave dinners. He said the guys at the fire station had chipped in and bought me the dinners. They said it would save them a lot of time and effort if I'd stick to microwave stuff.''

Crossing his arms and leaning against the wall, Derek asked, ''What did you say to the chief?''

Both Sarah and Alex whirled to face him.

''We didn't hear you come in, Dad.''

''I don't doubt it with all the giggling going on in here.'' He stepped to Sarah's side and gave her a hug, then turned to Alex. ''You didn't answer my question and—'' he looked down at his daughter and winked ''—Sarah and I are dying to know what you said.''

Alex pursed her lips. ''As I recall, I didn't say anything to him. But the next week after I treated one of his men for smoke inhalation, he invited me to eat at the station house.''

"Did you go?" Sarah's eyes sparkled with anticipation of Alex's answer.

"I did. And I'll be the first to admit, they were much better cooks than I. After that, I ate with them on a regular basis."

"Really?"

Alex held up her hand. "Scout's honor."

Throughout dinner and homework, Sarah's attention was focused on Alex. After the dishes were done, Sarah asked Alex to help her with her science homework. As Derek watched the two females working together at the table, his heart ached for his daughter. Sarah obviously missed the love and support of a mother.

Derek tried to ignore them as he read the weekly newspaper but the note of joy in Sarah's voice intruded into his thoughts. His divorce from Rhea had been ugly. She had wanted the house and car, but she hadn't wanted Sarah. Of course, that hadn't surprised Derek because a child would only inhibit Rhea's partying and sleep-over friends. He had understood that, but his daughter hadn't. All she knew was that her mom hadn't wanted her. While they were still in San Antonio Derek had taken Sarah to a child psychologist, but once they had moved to Saddle there had been no more counseling sessions.

Eventually Sarah had begun to smile again. But tonight was the first time since Rhea walked out that he'd heard his daughter giggle like the little girl she was. What worried him now was what would happen to Sarah once Alex's car was repaired and she returned to Houston. How long would it take for Sarah to laugh this time, or would she ever laugh again? And could he take that risk?

Yet, if he was honest with himself he would have to admit it brought a warm feeling to his heart to walk through the door of his home and hear the feminine laughter and know Alex and Sarah were in the kitchen cooking dinner. If he closed his eyes and used just a little imagination, he could envision them as a family.

The startling thought sobered him. There were two chances of his marrying again—slim and none. He had no intention of ever repeating that deed, and especially not with a woman who preferred city life to his world of west Texas.

"Dad, Alex and I are going to have a bowl of ice cream. You want some?"

Derek looked up from the paper. "Sure, why not?" As he set aside the paper, he realized that he hadn't read a word.

Sarah pulled out the half gallon of Blue Bell Homemade Vanilla ice cream and set it on the counter. Then she set bowls, spoons and chocolate sauce beside the carton. With a flourish she handed Derek the ice-cream scoop.

Derek couldn't keep from smiling. This little ritual had developed when Sarah was small. Whenever he was home, they would have ice cream together. She would get out the bowls and he would scoop.

"Dad's the best ice-cream scooper in the county. Probably in all of Texas," Sarah explained.

Derek pulled the gold cardboard lid from the container. Alex crossed her arms under her breasts and leaned back against the cabinets. "If he's that good, I want to see him in action."

Derek froze, the scoop buried in the vanilla treat. Her words brought a whole host of visions into his head. It didn't help matters that Alex's voice had a silky mellowness that would make any healthy, red-blooded male have caveman thoughts.

She must've noticed his reaction because she stiffened, dropped her arms and moved away from the cabinets.

"C'mon, Dad, show Alex how good you are."

Derek's eyes widened and he looked at Alex. Pink tinged her cheeks. When she met his gaze, that deep spark of awareness flared between them. Alex broke the contact first.

"Dad," Sarah complained.

"Okay, okay."

After dishing out the ice cream, the three sat at the table. Alex took the brown bottle of syrup and drowned her ice cream in chocolate.

Sarah's jaw fell open as she watched Alex's actions. Derek was as amazed as his daughter but simply shrugged his shoulders. A giggle escaped Sarah's mouth.

The sound caused Alex to look up. She followed the direction of their gazes. Alex set the bottle down. "I like a lot of chocolate sauce on my ice cream," she offered lamely.

"A lot?" Derek echoed, his voice filled with disbelief.

Alex's lips twitched as if she was trying to swallow her smile. "I'm not the bad one in the family. You should see my sister J.D. She really has a chocolate fetish. Me, I only have a mild case of it."

Derek rolled his eyes. "If yours is mild, I wouldn't want to see your sister's."

Sarah burst out laughing. Alex and Derek joined her. The joyous sound pierced Derek's soul and he realized how right it felt with Alex here and how tempting it was to wish that she'd stay permanently.

Damn, what was wrong with him? Hadn't he been kicked in the head by one female? Did he need to have it happen again to learn his lesson?

But Alex wasn't like Rhea. He couldn't imagine Alex cheating on her husband and deserting her child. No, he'd give the lady doctor credit for having a sense of honor, and he was sure she'd keep her promise to cleave only to her husband.

Unfortunately, in one way Alex was just like his ex-wife. They both disliked this part of Texas. He and Rhea had gone through all twelve grades of school together, but it was only after he'd finished basic training and come back to Saddle that they had seen each other in a different light, fallen in love and married.

It didn't take long for Derek to discover it wasn't him that Rhea loved, but the idea of getting out of Brewster County. He couldn't exactly blame her, because that same desire had prompted him to join the marines.

He'd accomplished his task and had seen more of the world than he wanted. Eventually he'd grown tired of moving every few months. When Rhea got pregnant, he knew he needed to provide a permanent home, and had joined the San Antonio police force.

In spite of enjoying the police work, Derek never felt satisfied, as if there was some part of his soul missing. When the job of deputy sheriff came up in Saddle, Derek jumped at the chance. The first day on the job in Saddle, Derek knew he'd found what he had been looking for all those years he'd spent wandering around the globe. He felt like Dorothy of *Wizard of Oz* fame, learning that there was no place like home.

Of course, he was sure that Alex had no desire to spend the rest of her life in this part of Texas, and he was through chasing rainbows.

Whoa, boy, he cautioned himself. *You're way out of line here. You're putting the cart before the horse. And in this case there isn't even a horse!*

A moan of delight rose in Alex's throat, drawing Derek's attention from his outlandish thoughts. Her eyes were closed and the look of rapture on her beautiful face affected him like a shot of Kentucky bourbon, going straight to his head and other regions of his body.

"Oh, that's so-o-o good." Alex sighed. "It's been forever since I had chocolate sauce on vanilla ice cream." She scooped up another spoonful and placed it in her mouth.

Derek couldn't tear his gaze from her face. Her lips couldn't possibly taste as good as they looked, but he wanted to find out.

That's just plain stupid, Derek told himself. He was buying trouble even thinking about kissing the woman. Only problem was, his body wasn't listening to his argument.

Sarah put her spoon down. A frown gathered on her forehead. "Why haven't you had ice cream? Don't they have Blue Bell in Houston?"

Alex and Derek exchanged a glance.

"Yes, they do. It's just that working like I do in the emergency room, I forget about some of the simple pleasures of family life. It's nice to do something so...normal."

"You don't have a family?" Sarah asked, her concern showing in her face and voice.

"Sure I have a family. A mother, father, sisters. The standard stuff."

"Are you married?"

Derek was becoming uncomfortable with the drift of this conversation. "Sarah, it's not polite to ask so many questions."

"Why?"

"It's not considered good manners."

"But isn't that what you do, Dad?"

Alex arched her brow, and Derek threw her a black look. He was trying to spare her feelings, and suddenly the tables were turned on him.

"The reason I pry into people's lives is usually because a crime has been committed, and it's my job to determine who did it."

Sarah rolled her eyes. "I know, Dad."

Sarah was teasing him. The knowledge slammed into him like a charging bull. She hadn't done that since before Rhea left. At the silence that enveloped the table, Derek glanced around. Sarah was nibbling on her lower lip and Alex was waiting for him to respond to his daughter's comment. They were worried about his reaction. He reached over and pulled her ponytail. "You're a stinker."

The tension in the room eased.

Sarah resumed her questioning. "What are your sisters like?"

"Sarah, didn't we just discuss not asking Alex any more questions?"

"I didn't ask about a husband," Sarah objected. "I asked her about her sisters, which she already talked about."

Children, Derek reflected, always knew how to bend the letter of the law.

"She's got you there, *Dad*." Alex's emphasis on *Dad* made it sound as if she and Sarah were collaborators in crime. His daughter made a noise. It sounded as if she swallowed a chuckle and it caught in her throat.

"My older sister is a lawyer," Alex informed them, "and my younger sister has a Ph.D. in ornithology."

"Ornithology?" Sarah's brow puckered into a frown. "What's that?"

"The study of birds. According to my dad, we're quite a collection of eggheads and pains in the bu— uh—" a blush stained her cheeks "—rear."

Derek could imagine the pride that George Anderson had in his daughters, all professional, well-educated women. He knew he certainly wanted to know more about George's middle daughter.

A warning sounded in his brain. This cozy scene wouldn't last and both he and Sarah would suffer when Alex left. And that was the fly in this ointment. After less than a day and a half, Alex seemed to have carved out a niche in his family. He didn't like the idea and certainly had no desire to put his heart on the chopping block again.

Abruptly he laid down his spoon. "I need to walk over to my office and check on those DEA agents at the ranch."

"But wouldn't Uncle Todd give them your home number?" Sarah asked innocently.

Leave it to a child to state the truth. Alex tried to appear nonchalant, but he sensed she was waiting to see how he answered Sarah's question.

"Sure he would, but I don't know if the guys in Marfa have my number, so to be safe, I need to go check." He stood. "Isn't it about bedtime for you,

Sarah?'' If he kept the time Sarah spent with Alex to a minimum, maybe it wouldn't be so bad later when he and Sarah were alone.

"But it's early, Dad. It's only nine."

"Right. Time to think about bedtime. If you get ready quickly, you can read until ten."

The gaiety in his daughter fled. Derek cursed himself, but this was the best way to handle the situation.

"Okay."

Why did she make it sound as if he was inflicting a terrible punishment on her? Derek leaned down and kissed Sarah's cheek. "When I get back, I'll come in and we'll talk."

From the corner of his eye he caught Alex's puzzled frown. He nodded to her, then escaped the kitchen. Maybe he could bury some of these fierce feelings in work.

After several hours, first at his office checking with the sheriff in Alpine, then driving out to talk to the DEA agents, Derek discovered he couldn't shake off his longings.

As he drove back from the ranch, he admitted defeat. Well, if he couldn't put Alex out of his mind, at least he would rein in his wayward body and clamp down on the emotions running amok in his head.

He was successful until he opened the door and found Alex asleep on the couch, two mugs of something on the coffee table. He peeked. Coffee and what had been at one time hot chocolate.

The significance of what she'd done hit him like a punch to the gut. She had tried to wait up for him, and although her spirit might have been willing, her body wasn't. Her actions blew his indifference all to hell.

For the first time in his police career, someone other than Sarah had cared enough about him to worry.

Damn and double damn.

He was in big, big, Texas-sized trouble here.

Through layers of sleep, Alex saw the most delicious vision of a handsome male hovering over her. A lock of hair fell over his broad forehead and his intriguing brown eyes were filled with concern. The man should be on a calendar somewhere so females all over the nation could ooh and aah. She snuggled into the cushions, ready to slip into a deeper sleep.

"Hi."

His voice jerked her out of her dream world. Her feet hit the floor and she sat up like a jack-in-the-box. Alex felt like a child, caught slipping out of her second-story window to go skinny-dipping with her best friend. "I guess I fell asleep." She felt stupid, stating the obvious. "What time is it?"

"It's close to midnight."

She stretched her neck, trying to work out the kinks and gather her scattered wits. "What took you so long? Was there some kind of problem?"

"No. It took longer than I thought to iron out the logistics problems with the DEA agents. I appreciate you being here with Sarah. How did she take it when I called?"

"She was a little disappointed but tried to put on her best face." Alex thought about Sarah's reaction, how she'd taken her father's delay in stride. But Alex had seen the hurt and longing lurking in Sarah's eyes. "It's happened before, hasn't it?"

He pointed to the mug of coffee. "Is that for me?"

"Yes."

He picked up the mug and walked into the kitchen. Alex followed him and watched him put the coffee in the microwave and hit the minute button. Alex wondered if he would answer her question. Of course, Derek's relationship with his daughter wasn't any of her business. But Alex remembered all the times her dad had promised to take her somewhere, then been called away by some business crisis. It had always hurt, and the bleak look in Sarah's eyes tonight reminded Alex of her own long-ago pain.

The buzzer on the microwave sounded, and Derek pulled the mug from the interior. After taking a sip, he looked at her, and she read his stark anguish. His failure to be here with Sarah hurt him.

"Yeah, it's happened before." He gave a harsh laugh. "The sad truth, Alex, is that of Sarah's two parents, I've been the one she could count on most." He shook his head. "She's a terrific little girl and doesn't deserve the parents she got." He brushed by her and walked into the living room.

His honesty was like a scalding burn on her already hurting heart. Alex didn't need his emotional turmoil. She had enough of her own. Her brain screamed out a warning that she needed to say good-night, and race to her bedroom, and lock the door. Instead, she joined him on the couch.

"The Bible says love covers a multitude of sins," Alex offered in way of comfort. Her brain was saying one thing, her heart and mouth another. And she seemed to have no control over what was happening. It was as if she was standing back and watching another person converse with Derek.

"What is that supposed to mean?" he tersely asked, setting down his mug.

"It means that if you love Sarah and show it, then you missing her bedtime now and again is forgivable. And from what I've seen so far, you do show it."

He shrugged. His manner was seemingly careless, but Alex felt his inner tension. "Yeah, I love her. She was the only decent thing that came out of my marriage." He stared down into his empty mug. "Sarah's been through a lot. Rhea, my ex, didn't much care for motherhood. For her, a baby was an inconvenience. She couldn't party and go out with her friends because she had to take care of Sarah. When I was working and couldn't be home, Rhea would leave Sarah with whoever would volunteer to care for her."

The emotions pouring out of him pulled at Alex, and as much as she wanted to withdraw into her protective shell, she couldn't and wouldn't. Tonight, sharing dinner and ice cream with Sarah and Derek had made her feel normal. Her reaction had surprised her, but she was grateful to Derek for the small miracle and wanted to return the favor.

"Sometimes when I have to leave Sarah with Mabel or my brother, I'm afraid she thinks it's her mother all over again."

Alex couldn't stand the pain in his voice, the bleakness of his eyes. Reaching out, she ran her fingers along his jaw. His head turned into her hand, and his gaze locked with hers. The dark hunger of sexual need exploded between them.

He lowered his head to hers. The touch of his lips was agonizingly sweet, making Alex want more. Her eyes fluttered closed and she opened her mouth, inviting a more intimate contact.

His tongue slipped past her teeth and she tasted coffee and the wonderful flavor that was this man. A longing so deep that it reached the very center of her being bubbled up in her, obliterating all reason and rational thought. The real world with its cares and fears fell away, and all she knew was the glorious touch of his mouth and the life-giving heat of his body. And the marvelous joy of forgetfulness.

Her hand glided over his cheek and into the thickness of his hair. She wanted to be closer to him. Her action ignited him and he caught her around the waist and pulled her onto his lap. Before she could protest, he cupped her face and took her mouth again. He wasn't gentle, the need in him giving way to a passion that seared them both with flames of pleasure.

Derek rained kisses down her throat to the hollow of her neck. When his warm palm slid under her shirt and covered her breast, Alex came crashing back to reality.

"Derek," she whispered frantically.

He went still.

"This is insane," she said. "We can't do this."

He lifted his head from her neck and looked into her eyes. Slowly she saw the fiery storm of desire retreat and sanity return. He still hadn't removed his hand from her breast, and the heat from the contact burned down into her inner core. It was heaven and hell to have him touch her.

"You're right." Regret touched his expression. Slowly, never lifting his palm from her skin, he slid it down to her waist, then out from under the hem of her shirt. He paused for a moment, and Alex felt the weight of his hands on her, then he lifted her back to her original position on the couch.

Resting his elbows on his knees, he fixed his gaze on something across the room. "Do you know, Doc, this was the first time since I've been a cop that someone was waiting up for me when I came home or—" he glanced at her, the corner of his mouth drawn up in a half smile "—at least tried to wait up."

Alex felt a trembling in the emotional ground beneath her feet. She heard the loneliness in his voice and identified with it. How often had she come home after an emotionally draining day in the emergency room to an empty apartment and longed for someone to be there and share the ups and downs of her day?

She started to reach out to him again, wanting to ease his burden, then snatched her hand back. She couldn't afford to risk her heart and allow herself to be drawn into this man's life. Instinctively Alex knew if she opened herself up to him, Derek would melt the iceberg surrounding her heart, and she would slip into the churning emotional sea surrounding her. And Alex feared she wouldn't survive in those black, choppy waters.

He turned to her. "Thanks, Alexandra."

The way he pronounced her name raced through her veins like a fine wine. Softly, sweetly, as if treasured by him. It warmed the cold depths of her soul.

She groped for something to say. "Your wife never waited up for you?"

His harsh laugh made her cringe and her mind instantly recalled the conversation they'd had earlier, before their mind-blowing kisses. "Oh."

"An understatement, Doc. Rhea had no use for Sarah or me. She was never interested in when I was coming home from work." Resentment and rancor rang in his voice. "As a matter of fact, when I was home, she made it plain I was in her way." He shook his head. "It always amazed me how I could've misjudged her character."

Alex couldn't resist trying to soothe his pain. "When people are young and in the first flush of love, sometimes they can't see clearly."

"You mean I was ruled by my hormones?"

"No, I wouldn't say that."

"I would. But I learned from my mistake and won't repeat it again."

"You aren't the only one to whom that's happened. I remember some friends in med school who were physically attracted to each other but never learned to be friends. Their marriage lasted six months."

He leaned back against the cushions of the sofa. "You should've become a shrink."

"Not me. I don't flow in the same channel as those folks."

His mouth curved into that grin that always tugged at her heart. He rested his arm on the top of the couch. "Why did you become a doctor?"

"When I was growing up, all I wanted was to be a person apart from my dad. I really didn't have an aim in life until the year I graduated from high school. That year my younger sister, Toni, was in a terrible car accident. She almost died because she didn't get immediate trauma care. She survived, but it took her years to overcome the injuries. After Toni's third surgery to repair her shattered legs, I decided I wanted to become a trauma specialist."

She brushed her fingers over the weave of the cushion, wondering if she should tell him the rest of the story. "My decision to be an ER doctor was only reinforced by my husband's death. He'd gone to visit his brother in Mason and was in a head-on collision with another car. By the time they were able to get him to the nearest trauma center, over a hundred miles away, he was beyond help.''

Tears gathered in her eyes. Alex took a deep breath, forcing back the moisture. ''It's late.'' She stood and Derek followed her lead. He was too close for comfort. She could feel the heat of his body and wanted to rush into his arms and have him burn away the dark memories that haunted her. But down that path lay insanity.

Taking a step back, she looked up at him. ''Good night.'' She hurried around the couch and started down the hall.

''Alexandra.''

The sound of her name on his lips was like the voice of temptation, low and seductive. She turned slowly, reluctant to face the devil who called to her. ''What?''

''Thanks for caring for Sarah.''

''No problem.'' She turned.

''Doc.''

She heard him walk down the hall and began to tremble. *Let me go to bed, Derek, before we both do something we might regret,* she silently pleaded.

He stopped next to her and lightly touched her chin. Her gaze flew up to his. He opened his mouth, then closed it, and shook his head. His fingers fell away from her face and he stepped away. ''Do you want me to wake you at six-thirty when Sarah and I get up?''

Relief washed over Alex. Apparently he'd heard her plea, or maybe common sense had grabbed him, because he hadn't pushed what had flared between them. ''That would be fine.''

She hurried to her room, aware that he watched her. She could feel his eyes on her back and wanted to look over her shoulder at him.

Don't do it, an inner voice warned. *It will only cause trouble.*

Slipping into the unlit room, Alex sank against the closed door. Her heart pounded with relief that she had escaped—if only temporarily.

But had she? What was she going to do tomorrow, when she had to stare into his deep brown eyes and watch his enticing mouth wreak such havoc on her heart? Would Derek be any less of a temptation in the cold light of day than he was in the deep hours of the night?

How long could she last against the sensual pull he exerted on her emotions without repeating the events of tonight? Heaven knew that she didn't need any more emotional complications, not with the jumble of feelings she was still trying to sort out. She still didn't know which end was up in her life, so how could she deal with a body that had decided to spin out of control?

She prayed she would last the seventy-two hours it would take to read Norma's test. Then she could leave Saddle and its snares behind.

Chapter 7

What the hell did he think he was doing? Derek wondered as he watched Alex scurry down the hall to her room.

Had he taken a stupid pill this morning or had he put his brain on hold while his zipper ruled his head?

He ran his fingers through his hair. The action called to mind Alex's small fingers against his scalp. Her touch had been like a red-hot branding iron, burning him all the way to his toes, vaulting him into a world where feelings reigned and there was no logical thought.

He rubbed the back of his neck. Of course, he'd acted like a bull after a cow in heat—no finesse, no technique, just groping animal instinct. He didn't blame her one bit when she pulled back. In fact, he was thankful she'd come to her senses, because he certainly wouldn't have.

And that's what scared him. He had vowed to never again fall victim to his hormones. Seventeen miserable years of Rhea's manipulation had been more than enough to last him a lifetime. He would never give a woman that power over him again. What he wanted from a woman now was a nice calm relationship that had a little fire, a little companionship, a little laughter. What he didn't want was this driving fire that Alexandra fueled in him.

"Ah, hell."

He shook his head, walked back into the living room and turned off the light, then made his way to his bedroom, shucked off his clothes and climbed into bed.

Folding his arms behind his head, Derek stared up at the ceiling. Well, he certainly found himself in a hell of a mess. Not only was he facing a probable epidemic with panicked people and no permanent doctor, but he also had a suspected ring of smugglers operating close to his ranch, bringing in heaven knew what contraband. And if that wasn't enough to give him an ulcer, he now had to face the most deadly situation of all: guarding his heart. It wasn't going to be an easy fight, because his body had already betrayed him and would probably do so again at the slightest chance.

This was a battle he couldn't afford to lose. Not if he wanted to remain sane.

Sunlight streaming through the bedroom window woke Alex. She rolled to her side and glanced at the clock on the nightstand. It was a little after ten.

A frown puckered her brow. What had happened? Hadn't Derek told her last night that he would wake

her at six-thirty? Rolling out of bed, she groped for her
robe and headed for the door. After washing her face
and brushing her teeth, she wandered down the hall.

"Hello, anyone here?"

Silence answered her.

There was no one in the living room, so she tried the
kitchen. A single mug and bowl sat on the table, a
sheet of paper next to the bowl.

Doc,

You were sleeping so peacefully that I didn't have
the heart to wake you. Help yourself to anything
you can find in the kitchen for breakfast.

Derek.

A sob caught in her throat, and she felt another
ominous shift in the icy block encasing her heart. He
had been concerned for her well-being. Her knees
turned to jelly and she stumbled into a kitchen chair.
Her hands trembled as she reread the note. He had
cared. Oh, boy, was she in trouble.

"Stop it, Alex," she whispered to herself. It could
have been Sarah who had not wanted to wake her, she
told herself, and not Derek.

Clamping down on her seething emotions, she fixed
a cup of coffee. This morning she needed the shot of
caffeine. After pouring a bowl of cereal she tried to
keep her mind on something besides the handsome
deputy sheriff. Maybe after she ate and got dressed she
would wander over to the post office and check out the
interior. If Norma tested positive for TB, they would
need to find the point of contact for the disease.

Yes, that was what she would do. And if she was
fortunate, she wouldn't have to face Derek until din-

nertime. And then Sarah would be there to act as a buffer.

The post office was the perfect breeding ground for the TB germ. The thick stone walls kept the interior cool throughout the brutal heat of summer, but it also kept the interior dark and dank. The small windows allowed little direct sunlight into the building and the overhead light consisted of a couple of hanging bulbs that had been installed in the late thirties. From the musty smell, the ventilation in the place was poor. If Norma had the disease, then this building would have to be abandoned until changes could be made in the lighting and air circulation.

"Hello, Dr. Courtland."

Alex turned to the young woman behind the faded wooden counter that ran the length of the room. On the wall behind the counter were cubbyholes that held each individual's mail.

"I'm Lorraine Mayer, Billy's wife. Norma is my mother."

After shaking the girl's hand, Alex asked, "How's Norma doing?"

"She's prowling around the house, anxious for the time to be up so you can read her test." The woman looked down at her hands. "We're all kind of worried about it."

Alex heard the fear in Lorraine's voice. It was a tone of voice that she had heard often over her years as a doctor. The patient or patient's relatives were wanting her to reassure them that they would get well and everything would be all right. Normally, Alex's heart embraced her patients and she strove to find the right words to comfort them. This time she didn't have the reserve in her.

"Whatever the result, we need to find out why Norma isn't feeling well," Alex answered.

Lorraine nodded her head. "Uh—I wanted to apologize for what my husband did to your car." She stared down at her hands. "He shouldn't have done that. It's just he was so worried about my mom. He loves her like she was his own."

At this point, Alex would cheerfully have strangled Billy Mayer. If he hadn't loosened that hose on her car, then she wouldn't be in this mess. Pasting a smile on her face, she said, "Don't worry about it, Lorraine. What's done is done."

"Yeah, but—"

A shout came from the street. "Help!" The yell came again. Lorraine and Alexandra rushed outside.

A man stood in front of the feed store, his face filled with alarm. As soon as he saw Alex, he ran toward her.

"Doc, there's been a bad accident. Fred's been hurt and he needs help." He motioned to her. "Hurry." He turned and raced back into the store.

Other people had gathered on the street, drawn by the yelling. The automatic response built by years in the emergency room kicked in and Alex followed the man into the building.

A cluster of people were gathered in the back of the room. A moan floated above the heads of the throng.

"Fred, the doc's here. Everything's gonna be all right." The man who had beckoned her pushed his way through the crowd. "Make way for the doctor," he announced.

Like Joshua parting the Jordan River, the bodies shifted, giving Alex a clear view of the injured man. Fred was sitting on a stack of feed, his right hand clamped over his left forearm. Blood ran between his fingers and dripped onto the floor. In the sudden silence, the sound of each drop of blood sounded like a drumstick on a snare drum.

Alex's eyes locked on the spreading blood on Fred's forearm and the widening pool at his feet. Suddenly she was no longer in Saddle, Texas, U.S.A. Instead she was in a small war-torn town in the mountains of Bosnia, looking down at the bits and pieces of the youth she'd spent days nursing back to health. He had been killed by a shell blast.

Panic beat at her brain and her stomach threatened to empty itself.

"Doc?"

Alex heard the voice but couldn't respond.

"Alexandra." Derek's welcome voice filled her head and the warmth of his fingers on her elbow brought her back to the here and now. She glanced up at him, then around at the faces in the feed store. They all wore an odd expression, one that said they wondered what she was doing.

"Can I help you in any way?" Derek asked.

She shook off the last bits of the ugly images. She couldn't help that boy, but she could do something for Fred. "Does anyone have a clean towel, shirt, something to bind the wound?"

Fred motioned with his head. "My apron up on the counter is clean."

Someone snatched the apron and shoved it into Alex's hand. She wrapped the white cloth around the bleeding forearm.

She turned to Derek, who stood by her side. "Help me get Fred to the clinic. I can take care of him better there."

Instantly he had Fred on his feet and they walked next door. The crowd followed.

"Everyone needs to wait out here," Derek called over his shoulder as he left the clinic waiting room. "The doc doesn't need any help from onlookers."

Ruthlessly Alex separated her mind from the haunting memories and concentrated on the injury before her. "What happened?"

"I dropped a screwdriver on the floor. It rolled under a roll of barbed wire. I was careless and didn't watch what I was doing and caught my arm on one of the barbs. Made an awful mess, didn't I?"

"Indeed, you did," she answered.

"I have a talent in that area."

Alex began to clean the wound to get an idea of how serious the cut was. "Although the injury's bled a lot, it's not as bad as it looks," she reassured him. "It will require a couple of stitches."

"I figured as much."

As she sutured the skin, Alex carefully avoided Derek's eyes. Had he noticed her moment of panic? He would've had to have been blind not to.

When she was finished, she asked, "When was the last time you had a tetanus shot, Fred?"

"Two years ago."

She stripped off the rubber gloves she'd used. "You're covered, then." Pulling a roll of gauze from the drawer, she lightly wrapped his injury. "Those stitches will need to come out in a week. I'm sure any of the doctors in Alpine will be happy to take them out for you."

"Thanks, Doc. I don't know what I would've done if you hadn't been here. The drive to Alpine is mighty long when you're bleeding like a stuck pig."

Buried in Fred's thanks, Alex heard the need these folks in Saddle had for a doctor. And that need pressed down on Alex.

"C'mon, Fred," Derek said, pushing away from the wall where he'd watched Alex sew up the arm. "Everyone out in the waiting room is worried that you're in here losing your arm."

"You're right." Fred slid off the examining table and gave Alex a big smile. "Doc, you're one fine doctor."

Alex was able to keep control of her unraveling emotions until the men left the room. Once the door closed behind them, her knees gave out and she crumpled onto the rolling chair. She held out her hand and watched the tremors shake her fingers.

You're one fine doctor.

Silent tears ran down her cheeks.

Fred's simple words lanced through Alex's heart. What was most poignant about the compliment he'd given her was that it hadn't been qualified. Fred hadn't said she was a good doctor in spite of the fact that she was a woman. No, what he'd said was she was a fine doc. It was the recognition that she'd striven for all her professional life, to be judged solely on her skills, not her gender. Now when that recognition had come, fear crippled her.

How could she be a good doctor when she had to beat back panic every time she treated a patient?

"Alexandra."

Without thinking, she put her hands to her face and wiped away the tears before she turned to Derek, who was standing by the door.

"Is everything all right?"

He studied her, a speculative look in his eyes. Alex wanted to squirm under his gaze, but she refused to give away any more of her feelings than she already had. "Of course."

A heavy silence hung between them.

She nodded toward the waiting room. "How did things go out there?"

"Fred proudly showed the crowd his bandaged arm. He bragged on how fast you sewed him up. He had everyone hanging on his every word."

Again, the need of these people crushed down on her, making her short of breath.

"I'm glad I could help." She busied herself with cleaning up the area.

"It's almost noon. Would you like to go to Mabel's for lunch?"

Alex wanted to escape the clinic so badly that she readily accepted his invitation, despite the fact she wanted to find a place to hide and regain her mental balance.

Alex regretted the decision the instant they walked into the restaurant. The people gathered obviously had heard or seen what had happened with Fred, because they smiled at her and nodded their approval.

Suddenly Alex had no appetite. "I've changed my mind and don't want to eat right now." She backed out the door. "I'll see you at your house later."

Without looking in any direction, she hurried down the street, praying that no one would speak to her. If they did, she might start screaming and never stop.

* * *

Derek glanced at Alex, who was sitting on the sofa reading a Tony Hillerman mystery that she'd found on the bookshelf across the room. Sarah had gone to bed, leaving the two of them together. The edges of the book were curled under with the death grip Alex had on the pages. It appeared every muscle in Alex's body was tensed so hard that if he said boo, she'd shatter into a million pieces.

Was she worried there would be a repeat of the mind-blowing kiss they had shared last night? He could understand her concern. It certainly had put him on edge. With all the commotion in town this afternoon, he and Alex had never had a moment alone to talk about what had happened between them the previous night. Maybe if he reassured her that there wouldn't be a repeat of the incident, it would help her to relax.

"I hope you didn't mind me not waking you this morning," he said, hoping to ease into the subject.

She jumped as if he'd fired his gun.

"You didn't answer the first call," he continued, "and I thought you might want the rest."

"Thank you," she mumbled.

Silence filled the room.

"Alexandra, I want to reassure you there won't be a repeat of last night."

Her brow puckered in a frown. "What are you talking about?"

It was obvious from her reaction that she wasn't stressed out over the intimate exchange she'd had with him.

"You mean our..." Her voice trailed off and she worried her bottom lip as the memory washed over her. "Oh."

What could he say, with his ego shot to pieces? Sorry my kiss was so wimpy you don't remember. Yet as Derek stewed over her reaction, it occurred to him that maybe there was something else preoccupying her. Was what happened today in town with Fred the center of her thoughts?

The accident had resulted in fallout for him, too. All afternoon people had stopped by his office to discuss what had happened to Fred. Alexandra had managed to win over those who had seen her in action. Oddly enough, no one had ever mentioned the few moments in the feed store when Alex had stood over Fred, frozen, her eyes blank.

But he had noticed it. And it had gnawed at him—along with his thoughts of kissing her—all afternoon. What had happened? Why had she hesitated? If she was an emergency room doctor as she claimed, surely she would have seen worse accidents than Fred's.

But what did they know about Alexandra Courtland, apart from the information she gave them? They had taken her at her word that she was a doctor, but they had no proof except for the parking sticker on her car, and that could be fake. He hadn't even asked for a driver's license, so for all he knew, she wasn't even who she claimed she was.

His cop's intuition told him that scenario was way off base. He felt Alex was who she claimed to be. But she was hiding something critical and he would rest easier if he knew what that something was.

Her actions tonight only strengthened his suspicion. Alex was wound tighter than an eight-day clock.

Her movements during dinner had been jerky and her conversation formal and brief. Since he'd eliminated his kiss as the cause of her stress, that left only Fred's accident.

Why would treating a patient with a few stitches cause an ER doctor anxiety? Thinking back over the past two days, Derek could see a pattern that each time Alex saw a patient, she became stilted and edgy.

She put the book down and looked at him. "Is there something else wrong?"

"I was wondering about this afternoon."

She visibly stiffened. "Yes?"

The word was hard edged, full of challenge. The tight line of her lips added to the picture of a woman ready to fight.

"You were very efficient and good. I must've had a half-dozen folks stop by my office, wanting to talk about you. They asked if I could maybe charm you into staying."

Her eyes widened.

He could identify with her surprise. He'd had exactly the same reaction when it had been first suggested to him—stunned surprise. He'd never considered himself a lady-killer and was amazed to hear that folks thought he could seduce her. "Yeah, it surprised me, too, that anyone thought I had that much charm."

She flushed and lowered her gaze to her lap. "And what did you tell them?"

"I told them you had a job elsewhere."

She nodded.

"I also pointed out that after nearly being hijacked, you were probably in no mood to make this place your home."

An odd emotion darkened her blue eyes. It might have been longing or hopefulness, but it quickly faded. "What was the reaction to that?"

"That's where my charm was supposed to overwhelm you."

The space in the room seemed to shrink to a tunnel that held only the two of them. He saw her swallow and knew she felt the current running between them. The power of it could have run the lights of Saddle and the surrounding ranches for years. Maybe that kiss had more effect than she was willing to admit, even to herself.

Alex's tongue darted out to moisten her bottom lip and if he hadn't been sitting in the chair, he would've been knocked off his feet.

"I hope you told them I wasn't susceptible to that kind of bribery."

The words hung between them, and suddenly they both knew they were a lie.

"I told them."

Her fingers worried the frayed edge of the novel in her lap. "That's good."

"There's something else I noticed while you were working on Fred."

Her head jerked up and she stared at him. "What's that?"

"When you first saw Fred in his store, you hesitated. Why did you do that? Is there something wrong, Alexandra? Is there a problem that I can help you with?"

She set aside the book. "Did you find fault with my technique?"

"You know I didn't."

''Then that's all that matters in the end, isn't it?'' She stood. ''Good night.''

He wanted to call her back, reassure her that he was a good listener and she didn't have to face her problems alone. But her reaction made it clear she didn't want to discuss anything with him. And, he noted, she hadn't denied that there was a problem.

Whoa, cowboy, a little voice in his head cautioned. *You're leading with your heart and it's going to get stepped on if you keep going down this path.*

That was true. But at this moment that particular road didn't look so bad. Especially if it led to a certain beautiful doctor.

Alex sat on the edge of the bed and took a deep, calming breath. She should've expected it, but had hoped that Derek hadn't noticed her freezing up at Fred's store. He had and he'd confronted her with it.

Oh, he'd done it nicely, but Alex had the feeling that he wouldn't let go of the incident until she answered him. And what could she say to him? I'm having flashbacks to the terrors of the past year in Bosnia? No, she wouldn't share that with him. It wasn't his business.

Alex stood, walked to the window and looked out at the mountains in the distance. They glowed in the bright light of the moon, taking on a magical, fairy-tale quality where there was only goodness and happiness.

Wrapping her arms around her waist, Alex found herself wishing the enchanting feeling would remain in the harsh light of the day.

Her last conscious thought before falling asleep that night was maybe she was supposed to be here, that what she had thought was a cruel twist of fate was the hand of heaven.

It was a disturbing thought.

Chapter 8

Derek didn't know what woke him. He listened carefully and heard a low moan. At first he thought the sound was the wind, but when it came again, accompanied by an agonized *no,* he knew it wasn't the wind.

Slipping on his jeans, he went to investigate. It might be Sarah. After the divorce, she'd had nightmares nearly every night. But it had been a while since that had happened.

He walked to Sarah's door and listened, but all was quiet. A sigh of relief escaped him. He was almost back to his room when he heard another sob. It came from Alex's room. Quickly he went to her closed door and lightly knocked.

"Alex," he called softly.

A moan answered him.

"Alex."

Still nothing.

He debated the wisdom of opening her door until he heard her cry in a choked voice, "No, don't, please, no."

Turning the doorknob, he entered the room. Alex's head was thrashing on the pillow and her hands clenched the blanket as she fought off some inner demon only she could see.

Sitting beside her, he lightly touched her shoulder. "Alexandra."

"No," she shouted, sitting up. From the glassy expression in her eyes he knew she still saw whatever hell she was fighting her way out of.

He grasped her elbow. "Alexandra, it's just a dream. Everything is all right."

As she turned toward the sound of his voice, her gaze remained unfocused. After several long moments the glassiness disappeared and she really saw him. A shudder shook her slender frame and she started to collapse.

Unable to bear the pain radiating from her, Derek pulled her into his arms. She resisted for an instant, then melted into him, wrapping her arms around his waist.

Her warm tears against his naked shoulder were like acid burning his skin, and made him painfully aware of the woman he held. He tried to ignore the signals his body was frantically sending his brain and tried to concentrate on comforting her. Instead, what his mind registered was the fullness of her breasts pressed against his chest, the softness of her cheek as it rested against his neck and the temptation of her lips caressing the skin below his collarbone. His mission of mercy was quickly dissolving under the heat of her body.

"Dad, is Alex okay?"

Alex jerked out of Derek's arms and swiped at her tears. Derek turned and saw Sarah standing in the doorway to the room.

"Yeah, she just had a bad dream."

Sarah moved her head so she could see Alex. "Maybe she would like some hot chocolate? Remember when I used to wake up with bad dreams and you told me the only cure was a cup of hot chocolate? It worked for me. Don't you think it would work for her, too?"

Derek's gaze met Alex's. "Would you like a cup of hot chocolate? You can hear from my daughter's experience that it's a surefire antidote for nightmares."

The panic and sorrow were fading from Alex's face and a quiet thankfulness replaced it. "That sounds like a wonderful idea."

"Good." He stood, walked to the door and wrapped his arm around Sarah's shoulders. "You want a mug, munchkin?"

She lifted one shoulder. "It might help me to go back to sleep," she answered with a sauciness that only a twelve-year-old possessed.

"I thought so." He looked over his shoulder. "We'll meet you in the kitchen."

Once they were out of the room, Alex hugged her legs to her chest and rested her head against her knees. She was still shaking from the aftereffects of the nightmare.

Another scene from Bosnia had replayed itself in her mind's eye while she slept. The young woman had been raped, and held a gun to her own head, wanting to kill herself. Alex had not been able to talk the woman out of it.

Shaking off the terrible memory, she climbed out of bed and struggled into her robe. Having Derek there had eased the raw edge of the dream, and she had gladly melted into his strength. It had been the first time since she'd returned to the United States that someone had been there to share her pain, even if he didn't have the slightest idea why she'd been crying.

As she walked to the kitchen, she heard Derek and Sarah talking.

"Do you know why Alex had the nightmare?"

"No, and it would be impolite, young lady, to ask."

Alex reached the doorway in time to see Sarah throw her dad an exasperated look.

"Okay," she muttered, her disappointment plain. Sarah noticed her and blushed. "Oh, hi." She flashed Alex a self-conscious grin.

Alex motioned to the pan on the stove. "I'm looking forward to this special treat."

"This is Dad's secret recipe." Sarah's voice lowered. "It worked every time I had a bad dream." She fingered the buttons of her robe. "I used to have bad dreams every night. But after Dad and I drank this hot chocolate, I could go to sleep." She glanced at her father. "It's been a long time since I had a nightmare, hasn't it, Dad?"

"You're right. It's been a while."

Both father and daughter looked pleased.

Derek poured the hot chocolate into three mugs and Sarah carried them to the table. Once they were all seated, Alex picked up her mug. "Here's to pleasant dreams."

The other two nodded and took a sip of the warm liquid.

"Isn't it good?" Sarah asked.

"Very good," Alex agreed. "Much better than I made last night."

Sarah gave her a puzzled frown.

Alex felt her cheeks go warm with embarrassment, thinking back to what had occurred between her and Derek. "I made some while I waited for your dad. And of course, you know my kitchen skills are very poor."

Sarah giggled. "You can't even make hot chocolate?"

"Now, wait a minute," Alex objected. At least while she was engaging Sarah in conversation she didn't have to think of her dream or her attraction to the man across the table. Of course, it didn't help that he hadn't put on his shirt, and she had to stare at his naked muscular chest. "I said this was better, not that I couldn't make hot chocolate."

That set Sarah off into another round of giggles.

"If you're finished, I think it's time for you to get back to bed," Derek told his daughter.

"Okay, Dad." She rose, then leaned over and kissed her father on the cheek. As she passed Alex, she paused and gave her a peck, too. "Good night."

Sarah's actions surprised Alex. Her wide-eyed gaze met Derek's. He looked as shocked as she felt, but his shock quickly turned to disapproval once Sarah left the room.

"Sarah's still getting over her mother's rejection," he said. "I wouldn't want to see her hurt again."

Alex gawked at him, unable to believe she'd heard him correctly. "What exactly are you suggesting?"

"Sarah likes you."

"And I like her."

"But if you continue to encourage her friendship, she's going to suffer when you leave in a day or so."

"So are you telling me not to be friendly with your daughter?"

He hesitated. "I know it sounds stupid."

"You're darn right it sounds stupid."

"Now wait a minute."

"No, you wait a minute." She stood so fast that the chair nearly tipped over. "I wasn't the one who asked to be thrust into this situation. I have a little more than twenty-four hours before I have to read Norma's test. I suggest you contact Billy Mayer and tell him to get his rear in gear and fix my car, then I'll be out of your life so fast you won't see my smoke, Mr. Deputy Sheriff."

With one final indignant glare, Alex turned and marched to her room.

Derek ran his fingers through his hair, then rubbed the tense muscles at the back of his neck. He had certainly made a fine mess of things. As his grandmother always said, "Who hit you with a stupid stick?"

"I don't know, Gran," he muttered to the empty room, "but whoever it was sure did a good job."

He couldn't believe he had asked Alex not to be friends with Sarah.

"You're a real idiot," Derek told himself. He shook his head, still stunned by his own actions. Yet, when he had seen Sarah's face light up as she talked to Alex and had seen her giggle in response to Alex's comments, a fear had gripped his soul that his daughter would be hurt again by a woman she cared for.

What made things worse was that this situation was in no way Alex's fault. She was completely innocent.

She'd been dragged into this mess kicking and screaming. If anyone was at fault, it was Billy Mayer. Yet it wasn't Billy who had just made an ass of himself.

Knowing he couldn't sleep until he apologized to Alexandra for his unjustifiable words, Derek made his way to her room and knocked lightly.

"Alexandra."

He didn't have to call a second time. The door jerked open, and she stood there with her fist on her hip. "What?" The fire glowing in her eyes told Derek if he made one wrong move, he was going to eat a knuckle sandwich.

"Did you forget to say something? Do you have another insult to offer me?"

Derek winced. She could wield words with as much skill as she had sutured Fred this afternoon. "I forgot to apologize to you. I was way out of line a minute ago, and I'm sorry. The only excuse I can offer is I tend to worry too much about Sarah." He leaned against the wall. "She's just starting to act like a normal twelve-year-old and to see her so free with you, I panicked." He lifted one shoulder. "I guess I've become a little too protective." He tried to look into her eyes, but found she was staring at his bare chest. "Alexandra?"

Slowly she lifted her gaze to his. The insistent current of awareness that always flowed between them suddenly surged. "Yes?"

"Uh—" His response disappeared from his brain in the rising heat. "I hope you'll accept my apology and explanation."

She seemed to snap out of her wandering. "Yes, apology accepted."

Pushing away from the wall, he nodded. "Then good night. If you like, I'll take you out to the ranch in the morning and you can spend the day out there with Cathy. She's much better company than I am."

"I won't get in the way of the DEA agents?"

"Not unless you decide to go with them on one of their searches."

"No, I believe I've had enough of law-enforcement officials."

"Ouch."

"It was deserved."

"You're right. It was."

She gave him a satisfied grin and closed the door in his face.

Derek went to his room feeling as if he had wrestled a wild cat. Well, maybe he had.

"Morning, Derek. I was wondering if you know where the doc is this morning."

Derek looked up from the DEA report and leaned back in his chair. He'd taken Alex out to the ranch after Sarah had left for school and had picked up a copy of the report the DEA guys had filed with his superior.

Charlie Weaver, an old cowboy from the Triple R ranch, stood inside his office door.

"Yeah, Charlie, I know where she is. She's out at my ranch."

"Why's she out there? I heard she fixed up old Fred yesterday and Terri's baby the day before. My lumbago's bothering me and I thought she might give me somethin' for it."

"Now, Charlie, Dr. Courtland is stranded here for a couple of days. She's not taking patients."

Charlie huffed. "I heard that she saw Norma. That's what her daughter told me when I went to the post office. Was she fibbing?"

Damn, what was Norma's daughter thinking? "No, she wasn't lying."

"Oh."

Derek wanted to explain to Charlie the situation that had stranded Alex in Saddle, but if he told the old guy, then everyone in the county would know within hours. And he didn't want to get Billy in trouble. Although, if he thought about it, Billy deserved all the grief the knowledge would bring him.

"Charlie, the lady's on vacation."

The old codger raised one shaggy brow. "Too bad my lumbago don't take a vacation." With a final harrumph, he stomped out of the office.

Derek walked to the window and stared out into the street. The nagging question of Alex's reaction to treating patients popped into his head. The more he thought about it, the more he worried about her. Something wasn't right.

Maybe he ought to call Houston and verify Dr. Alexandra Courtland's credentials.

He picked up the telephone and, after checking with information, called Ben Taub Hospital.

"May I help you?" the hospital operator asked.

Derek frantically tried to remember the name of Alex's boss, or at least who she *claimed* was her boss. "I need to talk to whoever is in charge of the emergency room."

"That would be Dr. Everett Carlin. One moment, please."

"Dr. Carlin's office," the well-modulated voice answered.

"This is Deputy Sheriff Derek Grey from Brewster County. I need to speak with the doctor."

"He's down in ER. May I have him call you?"

"I need to talk to him immediately."

"Let me call down there and see if he's available."

Derek had to wait only a few seconds before the doctor came on the line. "This is Dr. Carlin."

After Derek introduced himself, he asked, "Do you know an Alexandra Courtland?"

"Has something happened?" The doctor sounded anxious.

"No, not to her, anyway. Her car broke down in our town and she's staying here until it's fixed. I just wanted to check out her credentials. There's been a couple of incidents when she's seen people in a professional capacity, and she's acted strangely."

"Define strangely for me."

"In both cases she seemed very reluctant. When Fred sliced open his arm, she froze at the sight of blood. Now, it seemed mighty strange to me if she's an ER doctor that the sight of blood would make her react that way."

There was a long sigh on the other end of the line. "Poor Alex. I thought with a little rest she'd be okay. Damn."

"So she really is a doctor?"

"Yeah, she is."

Derek wanted to make sure they were discussing the same woman. "The lady I'm talking about is five foot five, reddish gold shoulder-length hair, blue eyes. She's a good-looking woman with a sharp tongue. Is that your Alexandra Courtland?"

A chuckle sounded in Derek's ear. "Yeah, that's our Alex."

Relief swept through Derek. Alex was the genuine article. Now all he had to discover was why she was acting so strangely. "What did you mean when you said you thought the rest would help her? I mean, I may have a medical crisis on my hands, and I need to know if Alex has a problem."

"What kind of crisis are you talking about?"

Since this guy was Alex's boss, he needed to know what was going on. "TB. The postmistress of our small town might have the disease. The post office is the main contact point for all the ranchers in this part of the county."

"So you might have an epidemic brewing? Well, I can certainly see why you'd want to know about Alex." He paused. "Dr. Courtland has worked for me for several years. A little over a year ago, she volunteered to go to Bosnia with the Red Cross. When she returned after her year, she didn't want to take a couple of weeks off like I suggested. Instead she went right back to work. It was a mistake. She needed time to decompress."

Terrific. He didn't want to be emotionally involved with Alexandra, but Dr. Carlin was pulling him into that charged world of feelings. "Why do you say that?"

The doctor hesitated.

"Dr. Carlin, I need to know what I'm up against here."

"The first hour in the emergency we had a teenager with a gunshot wound to his chest. Alex walked to the gurney and froze, then tore out of ER like the demons of hell were chasing her. I found her in the locker room, sitting on the floor, crying."

Although Dr. Carlin didn't label what Alex had as delayed stress syndrome, Derek recognized the symptoms.

"What happened?" Derek asked.

"She dried her eyes, then told me she was quitting. Now, you've got to understand, Alex's a damn fine doctor and I don't want to lose her skill in ER. But more than that, she's a good friend and I'm worried about her. Alex needs to talk about what happened in Bosnia, if not to a professional, then to a friend."

Derek didn't like the drift of this conversation. He was a professional, but not the kind Dr. Carlin was talking about. And he certainly didn't qualify as a friend. "Didn't the Red Cross offer counseling? Or at least recommend some?"

"I'm sure they did, only Alexandra didn't take them up on the offer. She always said that psychiatrists and psychologists were nuttier than most of their patients, and she didn't need the inmates of the institution telling her how to act."

Derek bit back a grin. He could well imagine Alex saying that. "Well, you've answered my questions, Doctor."

"If I can be of further assistance, let me know."

"Oh, you've been more than enough help." More than he wanted.

Derek leaned back in his chair and rubbed his aching head. He had gotten his answer. In spades. Alexandra had spent a year in Bosnia. No wonder she had problems.

Delayed stress. He didn't doubt she was suffering from it. He'd seen enough cops and firemen in San Antonio who carried with them the scars of their work.

It's none of your business, a voice in his head argued. And that was true enough. Alexandra had not
asked for his help in solving her problems. If it wasn't
for circumstances beyond her control, she'd be back
in Houston this minute and be Dr. Carlin's problem.
Instead, she was here in Saddle with him, doing
strange things to his hormone level.

Apart from his carnal desires, Derek felt an emotional responsibility for Alex. He'd seen too many
cops self-destruct because they kept all their feelings
locked inside. He didn't want that to happen to Alex.
Dammit, he didn't want to be involved, but he was.
The first time he touched her, his feelings had gone
beyond simple caring. He wanted to help Alexandra.

Since when have you become a psychologist?

A sharp bark of laughter escaped his lips. What an
irony. He was going to try to play shrink to a lady
doctor who didn't want anything to do with shrinks.
Boy, was he in trouble.

Alex ran the currycomb over the bay's flank. The
familiar action and the comforting smell of the barn
took her back in time to her teenage years. She had
loved her horse, Twilight. In the chaotic years of her
adolescence, Twilight had been her main solace.

"There you go, big guy." Alex gave the gelding a
final pat and stepped away.

"You do that like a real pro."

Alex spun and saw Derek standing at the entrance
of the barn. She returned the brush to its place on the
shelf.

"I ought to. I groomed my horse countless times
when I was a kid."

He walked to the stall and leaned against the wooden wall, crossing his arms over his chest. "What kind of horse did you have?"

"A quarter horse. Twilight and I competed in many a contest and won several ribbons."

"Do you still have the horse?"

"No. Medical school took too much time, so I sold Twilight to a young man who wanted to make the rounds of quarter-horse competition." Remembering her horse, she smiled. "They went on to win a fair number of titles and lots of money."

"Do you miss riding?"

The question caught Alex off guard. "Now that I think about it, yes, I do."

"Do you miss competing?"

"Now that's an interesting question."

"Why?" He gave her a quizzical look.

"Well, because I never thought about the adrenaline rush that I got from competing. I get the same intense and urgent feeling from a crisis in the emergency room as I did from competition." She gave him an approving nod. "Maybe you should've been a head doctor instead of a cop."

"Cops have to know how to deal with people. If we didn't, more of us would get shot."

"Good point."

He pushed away from the wall and reached for the bay, lightly rubbing the horse's nose. "Since I'm so perceptive a guy, you might appreciate that I noticed an odd pattern in your behavior with Fred and Terri."

She went still, dreading what he would say next.

"I kept questioning why so talented a doctor would be reluctant to treat a sick baby or freeze up when she saw blood, apart from just not wanting to spoil her vacation.''

''And what answer did you come up with?''

''I decided to check your credentials to make sure you were who you claim to be.''

In spite of his actions being the correct and logical choice, Alex felt violated. ''You did what?'' she growled through clenched teeth.

''I called Ben Taub Hospital and talked with your boss.''

Anger and indignation rose in her, like the tides before a hurricane. ''And you discovered I am who I claim?''

''Yes, I did.'' From his tone it sounded as if he finally realized what kind of a mine field he'd stepped into, but he didn't care.

''Why didn't you call Austin and check on my license? Or better yet, why didn't you call my dad? You would've loved to chat with him.'' Alex took several deep, slow breaths to try to regain control of her roiling temper.

''Alex, your behavior was . . .''

''Was what?''

''Odd.''

''Oh, since when did you go to med school? Gee, if you're such an expert in the field of medicine, maybe you should take the job the town offered. Then you could be the deputy doc.'' She was shaking. The tight hold she kept on her emotions was slipping dangerously out of control.

''Alexandra,'' he said softly. His eyes were tender with compassion and he held out his hand.

She slapped it away. ''Don't Alexandra me.''

''I know about Bosnia.''

His words held her paralyzed.

"Your boss was concerned about you. He said you might be suffering from delayed stress. I agree with him. You need to talk about what happened."

A red haze fell over her vision. She snatched the currycomb from the shelf and threw it at him.

He dodged the missile. "Hey, what are you doing?"

"You bastard, how dare you? You have no business messing around in my life." Her voice rose with each word until she was shouting. "Who gave you the right?"

"Listen, lady, I've seen too many good cops who kept everything inside. Eventually the ugliness and sickness of what they dealt with ate at their souls and drove them into hellish places."

"When you were sworn in as a deputy sheriff, were you given a divine appointment to muck around in other people's lives and set them straight? If that's so, maybe you should advertise for angels."

His eyes hardened as her gibe hit its mark. "You know I'm right, Alexandra. What you saw in Bosnia is inside you, festering. You need to face those memories and talk about it."

"Stop it," she yelled. "Stop it." She wrapped her arms around her waist and turned her back to him. She fought the tears. She would not break down in front of this man. Her gaze traveled around the barn, searching for something to concentrate on besides her oscillating emotions, and came to rest on the barn cat licking his paw.

Her heaving world was beginning to steady when the cat stood. It had only three legs. She watched the animal walk, with its odd gait, out of the barn. The pathetic sight was more than Alex could bear. She had seen so much worse and yet...

A sob tore from her throat. She struggled to bite back the next one but lost. Her hand clamped over her mouth, trying to muffle the sound, and tears ran down her cheeks.

It felt as if someone had reached inside her and ripped her heart out of her body, leaving her raw, bleeding and in agonizing pain.

"Ah, damn." Derek's voice filtered through her anguish.

She felt his warmth behind her, then he slipped his arms around her waist and drew her back against his strength. His chin settled on her shoulder. She tried to remain stiff and unyielding in his arms, but the comfort of his body was too powerful. Turning in his embrace, she wrapped her arms around his waist.

The dam broke inside Alex. The faces of those children and adults she had tried to help, yet failed, flashed through her mind. The tears she hadn't shed before now came with a vengeance.

"That's it, sweetheart," Derek crooned softly in her ear. "Let it out. Get rid of it all."

In the midst of her heartache Alex knew she could fall apart and Derek would be here to catch the pieces. She was safe.

Time seemed to stand still. Alex might have cried for hours or minutes, she didn't know. But when the last tear fell, she became aware of the hard chest beneath her wet cheek.

Derek handed her a clean handkerchief. "Blow," he commanded.

She obeyed, then dabbed her wet cheeks.

Derek cupped her chin in his hand and lifted her face to his. "Feel better?" His fingers lightly wiped away the remaining moisture from her face.

She nodded.

"I'm sorry I had to push you."

She sniffled. "No, you're not."

He gave her that heart-stopping, curl-your-toes grin of his. "It's all part of the job, ma'am."

Her gaze dropped to the strong column of his throat. Her feelings were too raw to look him straight in the eye. "Thank you for caring." She handed him back the handkerchief. He stuffed it in his back pocket.

"I'm up here, Alexandra." His thumb tilted her chin up. Although there had been lightness in his voice, his eyes were dark with awareness. His hand slipped to the side of her neck; his thumb traced the underside of her jaw, then found the pounding pulse at the base of her neck.

Suddenly Alex was aware of every inch of his large frame pressed against hers. The air around them turned heavy and charged, like the thick moments before a thunderstorm struck.

Derek's gaze settled on her lips, and her mouth tingled with anticipation. Lightning seemed to arc around them as his mouth settled on hers, short-circuiting every rational thought in Alex's brain. All she knew was the clean masculine smell of him, the glorious taste of him as his tongue slipped into her mouth, the solidity of his body.

Her fingers dug into his back. She wanted to bring him closer to her; she wanted more, needed more, had to feel him in every ounce of her being. He seemed to understand her unvoiced longing, because he shifted his legs, bringing her into the cradle of his thighs. Alex moaned in her throat at the feel of his arousal against her belly.

"What you do to me, woman," Derek gasped before nibbling his way down her throat. She tilted her head back in order to give him better access. When his mouth reached the top button of her shirt, his fingers quickly opened it. He kissed the newly revealed skin, causing Alex's heart to pound so hard she thought it would burst from her chest.

"Deputy Grey," a voice called out.

Derek's fingers froze on the next button.

"Deputy, you in here?"

Derek's head fell forward to touch Alex's and she heard him mumble a graphic profanity. She winced.

He rolled his forehead against hers. "Sorry."

"I share your sentiments. Only I would've chosen another word."

Grinning, he lifted his head and secured the buttons he'd undone. "You would've said?"

"Rats."

He threw his head back and laughed. "As I recall, Doc, you just called me a bastard. Now we're back to rats?" He leaned down and brushed a kiss across her mouth.

Someone cleared his voice, bringing both Alex's and Derek's attention to the man who stood inside the barn door. Derek's arms fell to his sides and he stepped away from Alex.

"Excuse me," the man said. "I don't mean to interrupt anything."

"Agent Collins, you remember Dr. Courtland."

He nodded. "Yes, I do."

"What can I help you with?" Derek asked.

"Stan wanted me to check with you. We spotted a wrecked truck off a little-used dirt road. The truck had managed to go into a ditch. We think it might be connected with that plane we were looking for the night before last. We're going out to investigate and wanted to know if you wanted to come along?"

"Yeah, I want to go. I'll be there in a minute." Once the agent was outside, Derek turned back to Alex. "If you want to go back to Saddle, Cathy or Todd will be happy to take you."

There was so much that Alex wanted to explain to him, yet she didn't have the words right now.

His hand curved over her cheek. Though he didn't say anything, she saw the questions and longing in his eyes. There was a multitude of issues between them that would have to be resolved. "I'll see you back in town," he said softly.

She needed some time alone to pull herself together. "All right."

He hesitated for a moment, seeming to want more. But there was nothing else she could give him at this moment, except—

She rose on her toes and placed a kiss on his lips. "Be careful."

"I will."

She prayed he would keep his word.

Chapter 9

The front end of the beige '65 Chevy Super Sport sat in the ditch. The rear wheels were suspended inches above the ground.

"That's the reason the driver abandoned the car," Derek said, pointing to the back tires. He had followed the DEA agents out to the remote spot on the dirt road that crossed three different ranches.

Agent Beavins, the DEA agent in charge, motioned toward the car. "Let's see if we can turn up any evidence."

In a matter of minutes Agent Collins pulled a marijuana cigarette from under the driver's seat. "Maybe this is the reason the driver ran off the road," he said, holding up the reefer.

"Could be," Derek replied.

There was nothing else in the interior of the car, but when they opened the trunk, they hit pay dirt.

Collins grinned. "Bingo."

The trunk was filled with eighteen duct-taped bricks and several boxes. Derek took the Swiss Army knife from his front pocket and sliced open one of the bricks. He pinched out a bit of the substance. "Marijuana."

Collins bent and sniffed the brick. "What else is in there?"

Derek pulled back the tape. On the back side of the tape was a blue sheet. "It's a sheet of fabric softener."

The three men looked at each other.

"Someone ought to tell the drug smugglers it's an old wives' tale about sheets of fabric softeners," Beavins said. "It doesn't throw the dogs off. They can still smell the drug."

Collins pointed to the unmarked boxes. "What's in there?"

Derek reached for the nearest carton. He opened the lid and stared down at twelve bottles. He pulled out one of the five-milliliter bottles. "Halotestin."

"Are they all steroids?" Beavins pointed to the other boxes.

"Let's see."

The next one contained pills. Derek read the brand on the plastic bottle, "Anadrol. Seems our smugglers aren't picky about how they get their testosterone."

In the remaining boxes they discovered several other anabolic steroids commonly misused by people who wanted to increase muscle mass.

"Now we know what we're looking for," Derek said.

"Partly." Collins closed the lid on a cardboard container. "Whoever is smuggling might bring something else in the next time. It looks like maybe they take orders, then fill them. It might be cocaine next time.''

"Damn." Derek took off his hat and raked his fingers through his hair. "There's no place safe anymore, is there?"

Beavins stared out at the horizon. "Afraid not. This poison is everywhere."

As he drove back into Saddle, Derek tried to pinpoint a place between the Grey, Moore and Schuller ranches where an airplane could set down. Nothing came to mind.

He turned onto the street where his house was located and hit the brakes. "What the hell?" he mumbled to himself.

On the left side of the street were four houses. On the right side was a flat field that ran to the dry creek bed. Parked across from his house was a black-and-gold helicopter with Anderson Oil stenciled on the side of it. If he didn't miss his guess, Alexandra's daddy had come to see what had happened to his daughter. The time to pay the piper was here. Too bad he was going to have to face George Anderson alone, because he knew without being told that Billy Mayer would be nowhere to be found.

Derek parked his Jeep in the driveway and climbed out. The helicopter pilot leaning against the copter's door nodded at Derek.

A booming voice greeted Derek as he entered the house.

"How long is it going to take to get your car fixed, Alex?" George Anderson sat in Derek's reclining chair, his white hair a striking contrast to his deeply tanned skin. Alexandra and Sarah were on the sofa.

"I talked to the mechanic today, Dad. The water pump hasn't arrived from El Paso. He's sure it will be here tomorrow."

"You should've called me. I'd have brought a water pump for that damn car of yours."

Sarah noticed her father by the front door. "Dad." She ran into his arms and gave him a hug. "That's Alex's dad," she whispered in his ear.

Introductions were quickly made.

George leaned back in the chair. "So, Alexandra, you ready to go home? I'll fly you to Midland and when your car is fixed I'll bring you back."

"That's not necessary," she quietly replied, but Derek caught the ring of steel in her voice.

"What are you going to do here until that guy installs the new water pump?"

"I won't be bored."

George leaned forward, resting his elbows on his knees. "You sure that all you're doing is waiting for your car?" He studied Alex, then shifted his gaze to Derek. "You know it's a long time since Vincent died. I wouldn't be opposed to seeing you get married again."

Derek's eyes widened, not believing he had heard George correctly. But one look at Alex's tight expression convinced him he'd heard right.

"That's not the issue here, Dad. I need to stay through tomorrow and read a woman's TB test. I can't leave sooner."

"TB? What are you doing testing someone for TB?" he demanded.

Her eyes glowed with icy indignation. "Because I suspect she has it."

"I wasn't questioning your call, Alex." George's voice took on a conciliatory tone. "I know you're a damn fine doctor. I was just wondering why you decided to see a patient while on vacation."

"I did it as a favor." She stood and kissed her father on the cheek. "It's good to see you, Dad. I'll call you when I get back to Houston." She turned to Sarah and held out her hand. "C'mon, Sarah, why don't we start dinner."

George gaped at his daughter as the two females left the room. "I didn't know she could cook," George muttered.

"She can't," Derek answered without thinking.

The old man's eyes narrowed. "How do you know that?"

The tone of the question rubbed Derek the wrong way. For an instant Derek considered letting the old man stew in his own juices. "Alex told Sarah and me."

George motioned with his head toward the front door. "Let's talk."

Derek followed the older man outside.

The instant the door closed behind them, George launched. "What's going on here, Deputy Grey?"

The old boy didn't pussyfoot around but cut straight to the heart of the matter.

"Exactly what Alexandra said."

"Alexandra?"

Why did her dad sound so surprised that he'd used Alex's full name? "That is her name, isn't it?"

That speculative gleam appeared again in George's faded blue eyes. "It sure is. But as long as I can remember, she's wanted to be called Alex. When I want to get under her skin, I call her Alexandra." He shook his head. "That girl was the biggest tomboy in Mid-

land. In the fifth grade she gave a boy a black eye
when he called her Alexandra.'' George placed his
Stetson on his head. ''You call her Alexandra often,
huh?''

The knowledge George had just imparted sent a
shiver of alarm down Derek's spine. How often had he
used her full name? And had Alex ever objected? ''I
usually call her 'Doc.' ''

George considered the response, then said, ''If
anything happens to my little girl, it's going to be your
rear in a sling.''

What did George Anderson think, that he went
around putting women in danger? ''*Nothing* is going
to happen to her.''

A sly grin curved George's mouth. ''You single,
deputy?''

Derek definitely didn't like the question but telling
George Anderson to butt out of his business would
probably cause more grief than it was worth. ''I'm
divorced.''

''Good.''

With that cryptic last word, George Anderson
walked to his helicopter, climbed inside and flew off.

''Well, what do you think?''

Derek glanced over his shoulder and saw Alex
standing behind him. Her anxious expression, the
furrowed brow and the worried bottom lip, touched
his heart.

''He's quite a man.'' It was as neutral an answer as
he could give her. He couldn't say what he really
thought, that the man was an overbearing SOB.

Her eyes met his, and she must have gleaned from
his face that he was whitewashing his opinion. A laugh
burst from her mouth. ''A creative way of stating it.''

The mirth died from her eyes and her mouth turned down at the corners. "I apologize for the unexpected visit. Dad called my sister J.D. and discovered where I was." She kicked a stone with her foot. "He has this overprotective tendency...." She shrugged.

"You could've gone with him."

"No, I couldn't. I gave my word, and I'll keep it." She started into the house, stopped and looked over her shoulder. "But if I were you, I'd make sure Billy Mayer fixes my car as soon as that water pump comes in, because I expect my dad will show up again in a couple of days."

The idea was mind-boggling. "I'll be sure to call Billy tomorrow."

He heard her chuckle as she walked inside the house.

"How are you feeling, Norma?" Alex asked. She carefully observed her patient's expression.

She shrugged. "Kind of bad."

"Are you running a fever?"

"Yes."

"You wake up in the middle of the night damp with sweat?"

The older woman nodded.

Alex pulled out a thermometer. "Open." She placed it under Norma's tongue.

Norma glanced nervously at the inside of her forearm as Alexandra measured the size of the reaction area.

"What's the verdict, Doc?" she asked, around the glass thermometer.

Alex removed the thermometer, read the temperature then sat on the rolling stool. "It's positive, Norma."

Norma thought for a moment. "What now?"

"We need to take a chest X ray. Since there's an X-ray machine here, we can take the film today."

They walked to the large machine located at the back of the clinic. As Alex loaded the film, she smiled at Norma. "You're lucky I know how to do this. A year ago I wouldn't have known how. But after having to do my own X rays in the field, I know what I'm doing."

Twenty minutes later Alex studied the picture of Norma's chest.

"How's it look?" Norma tilted her head to one side then another as she looked at her X ray.

Alex pointed to the area around the collarbone. "See this area that looks like a snowball?"

"Yes."

"That's the TB."

"Oh, heavens." Norma stumbled back and collapsed in a chair as if overwhelmed by seeing her disease. "Am I going to die?"

Alex sat beside the older woman. "As I told you before, in this day and age TB is completely curable. I'm going to prescribe a four-drug regimen for you to start on, but I'm going to need to do another test to make sure you're getting the right medication."

One penciled brow arched. "What kind of test?"

"It's nothing exotic. All you have to do is spit into a dish for me. Then I'll send it to a lab for them to culture and see which drugs kill the bacteria."

"I can do that."

Alex nodded. "I've searched through the drugs they have here at the clinic, and the drugs I want you to take aren't here. When I talk to Dr. Shelly in Alpine and tell him about your case, I'll have him send down a six-week supply of the drugs."

"All right."

"Now this is important, Norma. You need to take these pills every day, even after you start to feel good again. If you don't, your TB could become resistant to the drugs, then it will be doubly hard to find a drug to kill the bacteria. Also, a public health nurse will be assigned to your case. She'll check with you to make sure you're taking your medication."

"Is that normal?"

"Indeed it is. In Houston everyone gets a nurse. And if we run across a patient who won't cooperate, the district attorney can order the patient to a sanatorium in San Antonio for the year it takes to complete the treatment."

"You're pulling my leg, Doc." Disbelief rang in her voice.

"'Fraid not. I've requested the D.A. to send an uncooperative patient to the sanatorium."

"Oh."

"I was dubbed by one TB patient the meanest doctor at the hospital."

The corners of Norma's lips twitched.

Now that she had lightened Norma's mood, Alex decided to drop the other shoe. "I would recommend, Norma, for your health, that you stop smoking. If you don't, it's only going to slow down your getting well."

Norma's mouth compressed into a tight line.

"Have I gone from doctoring to meddling?"

Norma heaved a deep sigh that turned into a cough. "No, you're just telling me the truth."

"Also, the post office is going to have to be moved until you can get a better ventilation system installed and some different lighting for the building."

Norma shook her head. "I don't know where the money will come from."

"I think if the health department orders the place closed, the government will find some money to fix the problem."

"Doc, do you work for a public institution?"

"Yeah. Ben Taub is a county hospital."

"Then you know how money works in government. You can never get it for needed repairs and then there's always too much wasted on five-dollar paper clips."

Norma pegged it right.

"When can I go back to work?"

"Not for a while. You're going to have to stay at home for a couple of weeks until that medication starts working."

"You're kidding me, right?"

"I wish I was. But until you've been on that medication for a while, you're still contagious. Besides, you probably don't feel like going back to work."

Norma's eyes darkened with concern and she clamped her hands together. "I feel this entire mess is all my fault."

Alex laid her hand on Norma's arm. "You caught TB from someone. It just didn't spontaneously appear in your lungs. The person who gave it to you didn't do it on purpose, just as you didn't purposely infect anyone."

"Are you going to test my family?"

Now that Norma had turned out positive, Alex faced another dilemma. Almost everyone in this part of the county had come in contact with Norma, and if they had, they needed to be tested. Testing everyone would take days, maybe even a couple of weeks. How could she just hop in her car and drive off and wish everyone well? "Derek and I brought back several more tests from Alpine. I'll test Billy and Lorraine."

"Who's going to do the mail until I get back?"

"Your daughter-in-law seemed to know what she was doing yesterday. She could fill in until we know if she's positive for TB."

"What a mess," Norma muttered.

Those were Alex's exact sentiments.

Derek pushed open the door of the clinic. "Anyone here?"

"Back here in the examining room," came Alexandra's voice.

He made his way through the clinic and stopped at the examining room door. "How did your test turn out, Norma?"

"I got it," she said in a shaky voice.

Alex touched the older woman on the shoulder. "You're going to get well. Believe that."

Gratitude showed on Norma's pinched features as she looked at Alex. "I wish you were going to be here. I'd feel better if I knew you were close by."

Pain flickered in Alex's eyes, but it was gone so quickly that if Derek hadn't been watching her face, he would've missed it. But he knew Norma's remark had touched a raw spot in Alexandra's heart.

"Thanks for your vote of confidence," Alex calmly replied, no hint of her reaction showing. "But I promise we'll get you help. Now, you go home. I'll call Dr. Shelly and get your medicine."

Norma hesitated. She looked as if she wanted to argue but then relented. "Okay. Thanks for everything, Dr. Courtland. I know my son-in-law forced you into this situation. You've been great." Norma walked out of the room, then Derek heard the front door of the clinic open and close.

He watched the play of different emotions across Alexandra's lovely face. Anguish, regret, guilt.

"She only meant to compliment you."

"I know."

"You're doing all you can."

She nodded her head but didn't speak. After a moment he wondered why she hadn't said something.

"What now?" he asked.

Alex straightened her shoulders. "I report Norma's positive test to Dr. Shelly. Everyone who's been in contact with Norma is going to need to be tested."

A deep, cold fear slammed into his gut. *Sarah.* He knew the possibility was great that if Norma was positive, then she might have given the disease to Sarah. Faced with the reality, the horror and panic were worse than he expected.

He felt her hand touch his arm, then heard her soft voice. "Derek." He looked down into a pair of blue eyes that brimmed with understanding and compassion.

He latched on to her desire to comfort him. He wrapped his arms around her waist, pulled her close and buried his face in her shoulder. Maybe her warmth would drive away the fear eating his gut.

She didn't try to say anything. She simply held on to him, stroking his back with her small hands while he fought for control. Finally he lifted his head and looked down into her face. Her fingers touched his cheek, then traced his jaw.

"She'll be all right. Sarah's come through too much to let this stop her."

"Thanks, Doc." He didn't release her. She felt too good.

"Have you ever thought that you might have TB yourself?"

That caught him by surprise. His forehead wrinkled with a deep frown. "No, I can't say I have." Absently he ran his hand over her back. She made a choked noise and pushed away from him.

"Well, think about it. I'll need to test you along with everyone who's come in contact with Norma in the last month."

"That's going to be a lot of people."

"Give me a ballpark figure so when I call Dr. Shelly, I can tell him how many tests will be needed."

His fingers kneaded the back of his neck. "I'd say eighty, a hundred."

"Okay." She jotted down the number on a pad by the telephone. "When Sarah gets home, you'll need to bring her here so I can test her." Motioning to his arm, she commanded, "Roll up your sleeve. I'll give you your test right now."

"Will you have enough tests for Norma's family?"

Alex folded her arms over her breasts and studied him. "Deputy, don't tell me that you're afraid of needles?"

"Don't be ridiculous. I just thought you'd want to test Billy and his wife first."

"There's enough for everyone. Now roll up your sleeve and we'll get to work."

After Alex sent Derek to round up Billy and his wife, she dialed the number of the hospital in Alpine. "May I speak to Dr. Shelly?"

"One moment," the hospital operator said.

After a brief pause he came on the line.

"Dr. Shelly, this is Dr. Courtland."

"Ah, yes. How's that TB test going?"

"Norma Bolton is positive. As I said before, what makes this situation worse is that Norma is the postmistress and, according to Deputy Grey, the post office is the general meeting place for folks in this part of the county. They chat and catch up on what's been going on while they pick up their mail."

"I'll well aware of that particular habit of rural people, Dr. Courtland."

Alex would bet he didn't know diddly about rural folks. "The building that houses the post office will have to be closed. The stone structure is poorly lit and has abysmal ventilation."

"Have you tested immediate members of the patient's family?"

The man was a first-class jerk. She hadn't been treated as badly by a colleague since her first year in med school. Alex wondered how the man ever got to be head of public health with his personality. "Deputy Grey has gone to get them."

"Very good."

Alex ground her teeth. The pencil in her right hand nearly snapped with her outrage. How dare the man insinuate she didn't know the procedure set out by the CDC?

"Since you seem to have the situation under control, I wonder if you would consider remaining in Saddle for the year it would take to see these patients through this crisis? We both know that others are going to have the TB bacillus if everything is as you described. I'm shorthanded. I have no one to spare to go down to that part of the county."

Jerking the receiver from her ear, Alex stared at it, unable to believe she'd just heard what she had.

"Dr. Courtland."

"I beg your pardon. What did you just ask me to do?"

"I thought I was very clear in my request. I asked you to stay. I would be willing to talk to your superior in Houston to get it okayed."

Knowing she was about to lose her temper and say some truly choice things to the little nerd, Alex said, "You will need to send at least a hundred PPD tests. Also INH, rifampin, pyrazinamide and ethambutol are not available here. Please make sure you send a six-week supply for Norma."

The little tyrant sputtered. "Dr. Courtland—"

"Goodbye, Dr. Shelly." She set the receiver carefully in its cradle. "And if luck is with me, I'll never have to see you or talk to you again in my lifetime."

It took ten minutes for Alex to calm down enough to speak coherently.

"Alexandra?" Derek called.

She started to rise from the desk when the phone rang. "Back here," she answered, then picked up the phone. "Brewster Clinic."

"Dr. Courtland, this is Dr. Shelly again." As if she wouldn't recognize his voice.

"What, Doctor?"

"I've just spoken with Dr. Carlin in Houston and gotten his permission for you to stay for the coming year to see this situation through."

"You did what?" Her voice rang with steel.

Derek halted before the desk, his puzzled gaze fixed on her face. Alex could imagine her expression. It would probably frighten small children.

"I obtained a leave of absence for you from your job, so you can stay and work with me and the people of this county."

From his answer, it was clear Dr. Shelly didn't have a clue as to how angry she was. Well, she was fixing to let him know.

Derek placed his palm on the desk and leaned toward her. "Who's on the phone, Alex? And what's wrong?"

"Doctor, let me tell you what you can do with your offer. You can put it where the sun don't shine."

"Dr. Courtland, how unprofessional. But what could I expect from a woman?"

Alex wanted to roar out her rage. "No, doctor, let me tell you what is unprofessional. It's going around trying to play God in people's lives. You had no right to call my boss in Houston and obtain permission for me to stay and work for you for a year. What's unprofessional is expecting me to take over your responsibilities.

"And you better thank your lucky stars that I am a woman because if I was a man, I'd drive to Alpine and clean your clock. Now I suggest you get on the phone to Austin and get yourself some help."

"I will report your attitude to the head of state health."

"You just do that. And then tell Michael to call me. I think he needs to talk to the officials of this county about getting a new head of public health."

Abruptly the line went dead.

"Little worm," Alex grumbled as she hung up. She stared down at the phone, unwilling to see Derek's re-action to her little exchange.

"Alexandra." There was a note of amusement in his voice.

Squashing her embarrassment for losing her tem-per, she lifted her chin and met his gaze. "What?"

"You were wonderful."

Her eyes widened. "What?"

"You heard me. I think you handled that situation with just the right touch of fire and righteous indig-nation."

Not completely comfortable with his compliment, she tested him further. "You don't think I was a bit over the top?"

"Not if I understand what happened. Dr. Shelly called Houston, talked to your boss and hijacked your services for a year." At the mention of hijacking, he gave her a self-abashing grin.

A chuckle bubbled up in her throat. "You've got it right."

"Then he deserved exactly what he got."

All amusement fled and she looked up into his eyes. "Aside from the fact that Dr. Shelly has an emperor complex, what are we going to do?"

He stepped around the desk and pulled her into his arms. Alex went gladly into the welcoming warmth of his body. It was odd, but when he held her, the world fell away, and she felt safe and peaceful.

That had to be the silliest idea she'd had since she'd decided to paint her name on the water tower in Midland. She and her friends had gotten caught and had had to repaint the entire tower. To this day heights bothered her.

The notion of finding peace in Derek's arms was just as ludicrous. When she got too close to the man, he made her heart beat faster, her palms sweat, her mouth go dry and her mind suddenly go blank.

And yet . . .

"Doc, we're here," Billy called out.

Derek's arms dropped to his sides and Alex took several steps away from him. But in spite of the distance between them, Alex still felt the imprint of his body on hers. And in his eyes she read regret that they had been interrupted. There was something else there, as well. Something that reached out to Alex and wrapped around her heart.

"Doc?"

"Come back to the examining room, Billy," Alex instructed, moving to the door.

"Alexandra," Derek whispered.

Her steps halted and she turned to Derek. "Yes?"

"*We're* going to find a way out of this mess. Believe me."

His emphasis on *we* sent chills over her skin. "I know."

She administered the tests to Billy and Lorraine. When she was alone again with Derek, he asked, "Do you think I ought to drive over to Marathon and get Sarah from school and not wait until school's out?"

"Yes. And you'd better tell the principal what's going on. If Sarah comes up positive, then all children and teachers will have to be tested."

"This is getting more complicated all the time, isn't it?"

"You've only seen the tip of the iceberg."

An hour later the front door of the clinic banged open.

"Alex." Sarah's voice sounded odd.

She hurried out of the office and met the girl in the hall. Sarah stopped short and looked at Alex. The girl's worry was plain on her face.

In an attempt to lighten the tension, Alex teased, "Missed me so much that you came home from school?"

Surprise showed on Sarah's face, then a shy smile appeared. "Yeah."

"You ready for the test?"

Sarah lifted one shoulder.

"Your dad has already had his." Alex glanced at Derek and saw his anxiety over Sarah's reaction. "You should've seen how squeamish he was. I bet you can do better than he did."

Sarah's eyes flickered to her dad, then back to Alex. She leaned closer. "Was he really?"

Lowering her voice, Alex said, "He got real pale. I was worried that he might keel right over, in a dead faint."

Sarah looked doubtful.

"It's true. The bigger and brawnier the man, the bigger the chances are that they freak at the sight of a needle. I had this one man who was a lineman for the University of Houston Cougars. I had to take blood from him. This two-hundred-and-fifty-pound man went down like a tree when he saw the needle. Took the orderly out when he fell."

Sarah giggled. "You're teasing me."

"Nope. It's the truth. C'mon, let's go show your dad how to do this test."

"Okay."

As Alex fixed the syringe, she felt Sarah's anxiety return. "What class did your father interrupt?"

"Math."

"Do you like math?"

She nodded.

The clinic phone rang as Alex finished injecting the protein under the skin of Sarah's left forearm. Derek answered it.

"Yes, she's here. Just a minute." Derek held the receiver out to Alex. "A Michael Gigot is on the phone for you."

"I really must have made Shelly mad," Alex softly told Derek before taking the phone.

"Why do you say that?"

"Michael is the head of public heath for the state."

Derek nodded in agreement with her assessment.

After taking a deep breath, she put the handpiece to her ear. "Hi, Michael. What can I do for you?"

"Alex, why are you going around upsetting one of my minions?"

"I didn't know Dr. Shelly worked for you."

"It's something I usually don't go around bragging about. Besides, he holds a dual position with the state and the county."

"He's a sorry choice, Michael. The man seriously lacks a personality."

"I know, Alex. But getting doctors out to that part of Texas is no easy feat. And speaking of getting doctors out there, what are you doing in Saddle, testing people for TB?"

She gave him a quick summary of what had occurred.

"I agree with you that Dr. Shelly should not have taken it upon himself to try to get you assigned out there."

"You're darn right he shouldn't have."

"But, Alex, that health department is strained to its limit. They need more personnel."

"He can hire someone, if they'll work for him."

"Alex, I would consider it a personal favor if you would consider staying until we find the source of this outbreak. That won't be a year."

"But it could turn out to be a two- to three-month commitment."

"We both know that. But there's a big need, Alex, and you are the best person I can think of at the moment to handle this situation. Dr. Shelly doesn't have the experience you have after working in Houston."

A weary sigh escaped her mouth. She turned around and her gaze collided with Sarah's. Although the child was trying to appear mature and in control, Alex saw past Sarah's front to the worried child beneath. And at that moment Alexandra knew she just couldn't walk away from Saddle. She would stay until the source of the outbreak was pinpointed. By then if Sarah had TB, she'd be well on her way back to health.

"All right, Michael. I'll stay and screen the people out here and try to find the source of the infection. But you'd better find another professional to take over and manage the long-term care of these people."

"You got it."

"And one more thing. You tell Dr. Shelly to stay out of my way because if I see that man, I won't be responsible for my actions."

Both Derek and Sarah waited patiently for her to speak once she hung up.

"Well, guys, it looks like you're stuck with me for at least the next two months."

Sarah appeared pleased. Derek's expression was harder to read. It seemed to be a mixture of relief and worry.

Chapter 10

The sinking sun washed the land in hues of red, purple and gold. Alex watched through the living-room window as the lone figure walked through the open field toward the house.

Once they had eaten, Sarah had excused herself and gone for a walk. Her worry had been clearly reflected in her actions. She'd picked at her dinner, kept her gaze glued to her plate and given only single-syllable answers. The few times Alex had caught a glimpse of the girl's face, fear lurked in her eyes.

Alex stepped out of the front door and waited for Sarah. "That's a beautiful sunset." Alex nodded toward the horizon.

Sarah lifted a shoulder in a careless gesture.

Alex didn't let the girl's indifference discourage her. She settled herself on the porch swing. "There's something special about a west Texas sunset. The sky comes alive with color and makes you wonder how many shades of red God made."

Sarah glanced over her shoulder but seemed unimpressed.

"Sunset in the mountains of Bosnia comes much quicker. You don't see the sun sink behind the horizon. The mountains cut off the view."

"You were there in that war?" Sarah asked, settling beside Alex.

This is what Alex wanted, for Sarah to focus on something else besides herself. But it was going to be harder to talk about her experiences than she had imagined. "Yes, I was there, trying to save as many of the wounded as I could." Which were too few as far as she was concerned.

"Did you save a lot?"

Alex heard the unspoken plea in the young voice. *Please tell me I won't die.* "I was able to save as many as I could under the circumstances."

"What circumstances?" Sarah asked, apprehension ringing in her voice.

"Lack of antibiotics was the main reason. Some of the wounded needed more specialized medical care than could be given at the crude clinics I operated out of. Sometimes I could get them out. Other times..." She grasped Sarah's hand. "Those are problems you won't have to face."

Her reassurance didn't seem to satisfy Sarah. "Did you go by yourself?"

"Heavens, no. I went with the Red Cross."

Sarah outlined the edge of one of the slats in the swing with her fingernail. "Is it as bad as they show on the TV news? Brian Taylor says that it isn't as bad as they say. Our teacher says it is."

Alex closed her eyes and her brain was crowded with memories of the senseless, incomprehensible slaughter. "Yes, it's as bad. But what hurt the people most were the neighbors they knew their entire life turning on them and driving them out of their homes." Or neighbor killing neighbor.

The peacefulness of the encroaching night settled around them. Alex fixed her gaze on the horizon, trying to replace the scenes in her mind with the glorious close of this day in Saddle.

"When I see sunsets like this, I wish I had some artistic talent, but I can't so much as draw a decent happy face. I saw one of your drawings. You'd doodled on the edge of the newspaper that I picked up. I liked the horse. Is he one you own?"

A sweet smile crossed Sarah's face. "Jake is at the ranch."

"I know Jake."

"My uncle owns him but I ride him when I go out there. Dad promised me he'd buy me my own horse next year if I learned how to take care of Jake." A sob caught in her throat, and she turned anxious eyes to Alex. "I'm scared. I don't want to die."

Wrapping her arms around Sarah's shoulders, Alex drew her close and gently began to rock her. "Don't be afraid, sweetheart. If you have TB, you are going to get the best care available. You will have all the medicine you need."

"But why did it happen to me?"

Alex closed her eyes against the pain. Another young woman had asked her that very question before she killed herself. "I can't answer that. But look at it this way. Your guardian angel must've been working overtime, because he didn't let me pass through Saddle without stopping."

Sarah lifted her head, and through her tears she asked, "Do you believe that?"

A noise at the front door brought Alex's gaze to the man standing behind the screen. His gaze locked with hers, and suddenly Alex knew the truth of her last statement. Heaven, indeed, had brought her to this place. "With all my heart." She looked down at Sarah. "What you need to do is not worry, but be a positive influence on the others around you. I'll probably end up testing everyone in this part of the county. I'm going to need all the help I can get. And I want you to be my number-one cheerleader. Can you do that for me?"

Tilting her head, Sarah let her fingers pick at the fabric of her jeans as she considered Alex's proposal.

"You're going to be my number-one asset, Sarah. I'll be able to tell the other children how calm you were. If you can do it, they can do it. Will you do that for me?" Alex repeated.

"Yeah, I can do it."

Alex held out her hand. "Let's shake on it."

The edge of Sarah's mouth tilted up and her eyes crinkled as she took Alex's hand.

The scene unfolding before his eyes touched Derek. He'd heard the first part of the exchange and it had drawn him to the front door. When Alexandra took Sarah in her arms, something deep inside him eased. From this moment forward, he would never again see Alex in the same light. Sarah had needed her, and Alex hadn't turned away, like Sarah's mother had.

Maybe his confrontation with Alex yesterday had helped her conquer some of the demons that plagued her. Or at the very least, to face them.

But as grateful as he was, Derek was torn. On the one hand, he wanted Alex to comfort Sarah. Her reassurance as a doctor carried more weight than his as a father. He knew it had cost Alex plenty to share her time in Bosnia with Sarah, and he was grateful. But her actions made his dilemma even worse. The more Alex shared of herself, the stronger the bond between her and Sarah became. And the stronger the bond, then the greater the hurt Sarah would feel when Alex's replacement showed up and Alex went back to Houston.

And what about him? How would Alex's leaving affect him?

Maybe she won't leave, a little hopeful voice in his head whispered. As soon as the thought came, Derek remembered Alex's angry words to Michael this afternoon, informing him that as soon as they got a nurse out here, she was gone. Alex had never hidden her dislike of this part of Texas, so why all of a sudden did he think she would change her mind?

Love.

He jerked as if someone had punched him in the kidneys. Love? With what—or whom—was she supposed to be in love enough to hold her here in this part of Texas that she had so often said she hated?

Not wanting to answer the question, he pushed open the screen door. The sound drew Sarah's and Alex's attention as he casually strolled onto the porch. "The dishes are done." He leaned against one of the columns supporting the porch roof. "If Alex is going to be staying with us for a while, I think we need to make up a schedule for doing dishes."

Sarah's mouth dropped open in surprise. "Dad, you're going to make her do dishes?"

"The chores still need to be done even if we have company."

"Your father's right, Sarah," Alex replied. "If I stay with you all, then I need to help around the house."

Derek rubbed his chin. "I guess we could let Alexandra cook, but I don't think we want that." He turned to Alex. "Am I right? Do you want to cook or wash dishes?"

Her brow arched in surprise. "For all our health, I'll do dishes. My reputation as a doctor might suffer if I gave everyone food poisoning. But I can do laundry, dust, sweep. I'll even volunteer to do the bathroom."

"Good," Sarah said, clapping her hands. "You can have it."

Derek looked at Alex. "You sure you want that job?"

"I don't have a squeamish stomach, not working where I do."

"All right, then." He pushed away from the porch column. "Why don't we go inside and make out a schedule for the next few weeks."

"I'm going to need your help, Derek," Alex said. She looked up from the tablet she had in her lap to where Derek sat in his recliner.

"Sure." He set the remote control for the television on the coffee table.

Sarah had gone to bed and Alex had spent the time since planning her testing strategy. "Once I get the PPD tests from Alpine—which I hope will be tomorrow—I'll need to start testing everyone in town who's come in contact with Norma."

He rested his elbows on his knees. "Yes?"

"How do you suggest I get the message out to everyone to come by the clinic and be tested?"

The corner of his mouth curled up and his dimple appeared in his cheek. Now that her outrage over Dr. Shelly's actions had died down and she could think clearly, it occurred to Alex she was going to be stuck here in this house with Derek. And that was buying trouble by the peck as her daddy always said.

"This is a small town, Alexandra. Probably everyone knows about Norma having TB and that you will be testing the rest of us. I think they'll show up on the clinic doorstep without any prodding."

The sound of her name on his lips sent shivers of pleasure through her body. She'd never much cared for her full name, always preferring to be called Alex. But when Derek said her name, with the seductive roughness of his voice, it sounded right for the first time in her life.

The enticing pull this man had over her senses was growing at an exponential rate. She knew whenever he entered a room. She was always aware of his movements, even as she tried to ignore him. The wanting to be held by him, which she was trying to suppress, was growing. If she had to spend a couple of months here in close proximity to him, she didn't know what would happen.

Oh, yes, you do, her conscience whispered. *You know exactly what will happen.* And the frightening part was that she didn't find it scary.

He tilted his head to the side. "Is something wrong?"

Alex could've kicked herself for staring at him. "No."

He nodded, but in the depths of his brown eyes Alex found an answering fascination. She was in big-time trouble here. She felt like a piece of flotsam caught in a whirlpool, unable to control any of the events swirling around her.

"I need more of a plan than just hoping everyone will show up. My med-school professor who taught epidemiology would have a cardiac arrest if I left my strategy to fate. It would be like you sitting in your office, hoping those smugglers turn themselves in."

"Ouch," he said with a mock frown on his face. "I guess you told me."

"You deserved it."

"You're right. Tomorrow morning I'll go with you to every business in town and we'll explain the situation to them."

Alex glanced at her notes. "Also, I'll need to tell Lorraine to send anyone who picks up their mail to me for testing."

"Those who come into town can alert the others on the ranches to drive in and be tested."

"That follow-up can wait until I've read the contact person's reaction and know if they're positive or negative."

"It's not going to matter, Alexandra, because everyone on those ranches has been into town to pick up the mail, or get feed for their livestock, or pick up groceries."

She heaved a deep sigh. "I know. That's what makes this such a mess."

She ran her hands through her hair several times. When she glanced up, she found Derek staring at her unbound hair. His gaze found hers, then drifted to her mouth. Her lips tingled and she leaned forward, wanting to taste his kiss again.

The sound of a shot from the drama on the TV broke the intimate moment. "The health department is going to want me to try to find the source of this outbreak."

"How do you do that?"

"By process of elimination, which I'm sure as a cop you'll appreciate. It's like throwing a pebble into a lake and watching the outgoing concentric circles. Norma's the first confirmed case we have. We test all of her immediate family or the household. If they turn up positive, we test their working associates, each time getting a bigger ring. When the number of positive cases is lower than ten percent, we know this is not the source of the germ. If it's higher than thirty percent, we know we've found a contact point."

"Do you think just one person is responsible for this or do you think there are several sources of the disease?"

"I don't know. There was a shipbuilding town in Maine where one man infected everyone. CDC was able to track him down as the source. I hope I can do that here." She stood. "I think I'll go to bed. Tomorrow is going to be a long day."

"Alexandra." He rose to his feet.

She looked up into his handsome face, which was a definite mistake since she was trying to avoid further entanglements with him. He stole her breath away. What was it about this man that caused that over-the-top reaction in her? Derek wasn't the most handsome male she'd ever seen, or the smartest, or had the best body. So what was it?

Chemistry. That's what it had to be. That and hormones. And yet, there seemed to be more.

She had never subscribed to the theory that there was just one special man for a woman. But here this man was shooting holes in her theory.

His hand came up and cupped the side of her head. The bolt of electricity that ran through her nearly brought her to her knees. His thumb ran over the line of her jaw.

"Thanks for helping Sarah. I know she's frightened, and you eased her fears."

Alex had to concentrate to make sense of what he said. "I was glad to do it. It's part of being a doctor."

His thumb stopped its movement and his eyes darkened. "I don't think so. I can't see Dr. Shelly doing for Sarah what you did."

"He's an idiot."

"Granted." His thumb found the corner of her mouth. "But I know some of your secrets, Alexandra. It cost you to tell her about Bosnia to get her mind off herself. And for that, you will have my eternal gratitude."

She would've settled for his kiss. It wasn't smart or wise, but at this point her brain wasn't working.

As if he heard her, he leaned down and covered her mouth with his. Each time their lips met, it was sweeter and more drugging than the last. Alex moaned at the pleasure rippling through every part of her body. His tongue slipped past her teeth to duel with her tongue as more shivers of delight coursed through her. Beyond the ecstasy, Derek's actions touched a part of her heart that Alex had kept hidden and protected since her husband's death years before.

Derek's free arm slipped around her waist and drew her to his body. Alex felt like warm butter, melting against him.

"Sweet," Derek whispered as he tilted her head to the side and trailed kisses across her cheek. He lightly bit her ear, then laved it with his tongue. "You are so sweet," he murmured before recapturing her mouth. His hand moved down her neck over her shoulder to settle on her breast. The heated contact made her gasp. Her breast grew heavy, and she longed to feel his hand on her naked skin.

Fumbling, he tried to pull her T-shirt from her jeans. After wrestling with the material, he succeeded in freeing her shirt and his warm palms on the skin of her back were like heated irons. Sliding his hands up her back, he unhooked her bra and his hands slipped around her sides to cover her breasts. The shock and joy of the contact shot through her. In an instant of blinding insight Alex knew if this went any further, that little part of her heart that still remained intact would be pierced. And when she returned home to Houston, it would shatter. Could she run that risk, to try to live with her heart in pieces the rest of her life?

Fear swamped the passion, snuffing it out. She stepped away from him and tugged down her shirt. Derek's eyes sought hers, questioning her action.

She stuffed her T-shirt into her jeans. "I think I'd better go to bed."

"Alexandra."

"Derek, I'm not ready for this. I'm sorry."

The jangle of the phone broke into the uncomfortable silence.

Derek answered it. "Hi, Fred. Yes, it's true. The doc wants you and Carole to come by the clinic to be tested for TB, but come by late in the day to make sure the stuff has arrived from Alpine. Also, spread the word to your customers. Anyone who's been in contact with Norma needs to be tested."

Derek stared at Alex while he listened to Fred's response.

"Dr. Courtland is going to stay here for a while to test everyone and help get things settled. She's staying until county health can get a replacement."

Derek smiled and Alex wondered what Fred had said to get that grin. "All right. Goodbye." He hung up. "What did I tell you? Word spreads quickly in a small town."

"What did Fred say that made you smile?"

"He pointed out that since you were staying here, he wouldn't have to drive to Alpine to have his stitches taken out."

"I'd say Fred's a practical guy."

He shifted his weight from one leg to the other, drawing her gaze to his hips. There wasn't a spare ounce of fat on his lean frame.

Alex jerked her gaze and thoughts from that treacherous path. She gave him a forced smile. "Good night."

She hurried down the hall, running away from the desire her heart wanted to embrace but her head rejected.

* * *

Derek punched his pillow, hoping to find a more comfortable position. He hadn't had a decent night's sleep since Billy Mayer had disabled Alex's car. He ought to take out his frustration on Billy's hide, but was it his friend's fault that Derek was attracted to Alexandra Courtland in a way that he'd not been attracted to any other woman?

No, Billy wasn't to blame for Derek's hormones that had come back to life with a burning vengeance.

Turning onto his back, he stared up at the ceiling. The patch of plaster above his bed was becoming as familiar to him as the back of his hand.

As he was following the hairline crack around the room, an odd sound caught his attention. He closed his eyes and listened. The sound came again, and Derek recognized it as a muffled sob. Putting on his jeans, he went to investigate, worried that Sarah was still upset.

The instant he opened his door he heard the sound coming from the kitchen. With a frown he walked down the hall. When he reached the kitchen, he saw Alex, her back to the door. A pan of something was on the stove, but she wasn't paying attention to it as it smoked. Instead, one of her arms was wrapped around her waist, the other across her chest, her hand covering her mouth.

He came up behind her, reached for the knob on the stove and turned off the burning milk. After removing the pan from the burner, he rested his hand on her back. "Since you're in here burning milk, it's my guess you had a bad dream." He hoped his humor would ease the situation.

She hiccuped and he couldn't tell if she laughed or was still crying.

He bent to get a look at her face. "Alexandra? Are you all right?"

Her hand trembled over her mouth and her eyes were bright with turmoil.

"Ah, sweetheart," he said, reaching for her. He turned her in his arms and cradled her head on his shoulder, rocking her back and forth. "What is it, sweetheart? What's wrong? Was it a dream?"

She shook her head.

"What, Alexandra? Tell me."

"I couldn't sleep." She sniffled and Derek gently tucked several strands of hair behind her ear. "I got to thinking about Sarah. There were so many kids this last year I couldn't save." Her voice broke and her body shuddered with her grief.

"Sweetheart, although you're a skilled doctor, you're not God. There are things beyond your control."

"But there's this fear inside me that I could've done something else. Now, when I look at Sarah, I find myself doubting whether or not I'm the best person for this job." She buried her face against his shoulder.

Derek felt her warm breath on his naked chest. "Alexandra, tell me about one of the people you think you could've saved."

"There was a little boy. He'd just had his fifth birthday when a bomb hit a few feet from him. He lost a leg and several fingers."

"You operated?"

"Yes."

"Why did he die?"

"From the infection caused by the wounds. I didn't have any antibiotics to give him."

"Would you have given the child the medicine if you'd had it?"

Her head jerked up and she stared at him in amazement. "Of course."

"Then you did all you could."

As she considered his words, Derek read the guilt that crushed her heart. "Let go of it, Alexandra. The guilt will only hurt you."

She searched his face, and he felt her reaching into his heart, seeking the assurance, acceptance and the love she needed. He didn't draw back, didn't try to hide the desire he had for her, but let her see all that was there.

A single tear rolled down her cheek. "I don't know if I can."

Her broken cry spurred him into action. He kissed the corner of her eye, tasting the salty wetness on her skin. "Yes, you can, sweetheart." His mouth caught hers, and all he knew was that she needed him and that he would give her anything she needed. Even his heart.

His lips devoured hers, wanting to replace grief with passion. She came alive in his arms. Her hand roved over his back, then skimmed around to run through the hair on his chest. Her nails raked over his nipples, bringing a jolt of delight.

She wrenched her mouth away from his and kissed the pulsing column of his neck, then lower until her lips grazed his sensitized nipple.

"Ah, sweet, you don't know what you're doing to me."

Her only response was to slide her hands into the waistband of his jeans. His hands clamped over hers.

"Alexandra, are you sure you want this?"

She looked up at him. The expression in her eyes was like a drowning victim pleading for a lifeline. And he couldn't deny her.

Sweeping her up into his arms, he carried her to his bedroom. Tenderly he laid her on the bed, then slipped off his jeans before stretching out beside her. His desire for her was obvious, and he wanted her to see him, to make sure this was what she wanted.

When she reached for that part of him, he no longer doubted her decision.

"Whoa, sweetheart. I want you along with me when I experience that glimpse of heaven."

He untied her robe and removed it from her shoulders. He kissed the smooth skin at the cap of her shoulder, then followed the material down her arm. The inside of her elbow seemed particularly sensitive, bringing a moan from her mouth as he licked and taunted the skin.

Once he had the robe off, he caught the hem of her nightgown and tugged it over her head. She squirmed, helping him get the nightgown from under her body. Her actions only brought her body closer to his, her feminine curves cradling his harder masculine ones.

Derek placed his hand on her abdomen to stop the motion. His control was quickly slipping away from him. If she wiggled one more time, it would be all over.

She looked up at him, her eyes dark with hunger, and held out her hand to him. "Derek, I need you."

Her skin was smooth, like the finest satin. As he covered her body with his, the heat from their bodies mingled. It was like being plunged into a pool of fire.

Her hands roved over his back and her legs moved restlessly under him.

With a wildness that had never gripped him before, Derek's mouth mated with hers. She met his masculine fierceness with an equally strong feminine one. His mouth moved down her neck, kissing and nipping, to the sweet mounds that tempted him.

As his mouth settled over her breast, Alex moaned and speared her fingers through his hair, holding him close.

The intensity of her reaction rocked him. He felt the need of her heart as if it was his own.

Her head moved back and forth on the pillow. "Derek?"

He looked up from her breast. "Yes?"

"Now," she gasped.

After testing to make sure she was ready, he moved up her body. Slowly he entered her. It was sweet and powerful and shook him to his core.

He paused, trying to maintain his fragile control on his passion.

He heard her soft pants. Her hands cupped his face and brought it to hers. As their lips dueled, his body began to move within hers. Her fingers found his and interlaced. As the tension in her body rose, her fingers tensed around his until she reached the shattering peak of fulfillment.

Wrenching her mouth from his, she gasped with pleasure. It was enough to push him over the edge to join her in the small piece of heaven that held only the two of them. He rested his forehead on hers, trying to catch his breath.

Alexandra's mind reeled with the magnitude of what had just happened. She had awakened from a disturbing dream that she couldn't remember, and had lain awake thinking about the situation in Saddle. Then the doubts about her skill and ability as a doctor had begun to batter her. She had gone to the kitchen, hoping some hot milk would ease the panic.

And into that darkness Derek had come. Challenging her doubts and giving her passion for her pain. Joy for grief.

"What are you thinking?"

Alex's eyes met his. He'd been studying her and had probably seen every thought she'd had.

She slipped her arms around his neck. "You."

"Yeah, what about me?"

"That you're incredible."

He started to roll off her, but she said, "Don't leave me."

"I must be crushing you."

"No. It's welcome."

He rested his weight on his elbows. "Now, what was it about me that you think is incredible?"

"Your technique."

"C'mon, Doc, let's get more specific."

"Are you fishing for a compliment?"

"It's been a long time since I've done this. A little stroking wouldn't hurt."

The inner muscles of her woman's core contracted. His eyes widened then darkened. "Is that the kind of stroking you were talking about?"

He nipped her neck and she felt him harden inside her.

"Oh."

"You started this," he growled against her ear. "Can you finish it?"

"Just watch me." Then she proceeded to show him.

* * *

Much later, as she lay cradled within the warmth of his arms, Alex felt a small blossom of hope come to life in her heart. A long time ago she had given up the dream of love and forever-after happiness. Now, after sharing this extraordinary loving with Derek, that hope was resurrected.

And she didn't know whether to rejoice or cry. If she grasped that tender bloom and it died, there would be nothing left of her heart. But if it grew and survived, what then?

"Your mind is running at full speed again, sweetheart."

She turned her head toward his. "What makes you say that?"

His forefinger lightly traced over the area between her eyebrows. "I've noticed that when you're thinking or worried, the skin here wrinkles. It's cute, but a dead giveaway."

She couldn't recall the last time she'd been called cute. "I'm still in awe of what happened here."

As his hand stroked over her face and down her neck, a large, satisfied grin pulled at his lips.

"Don't let this go to your head," she admonished him.

"Too late. You've done wonders for my ego."

Alex remembered his earlier comment about how long it had been since he'd made love to a woman. She couldn't help being curious. "You mentioned that it's been a while since..."

One brow arched as he waited for her to complete her thought. "Yes?" Mischief lurked in his eyes.

Suddenly her courage deserted her. "Nothing."

"Are you wondering how long it's been since I made love to a woman?"

She was mortified by her nosiness. "It's none of my business. I shouldn't have asked."

He lightly kissed the corner of her mouth. "The last woman I made love to was my ex-wife." His expression turned grim as he recalled that final encounter. "It wasn't so much lovemaking as it was a way to release anger. It left a bad taste in my mouth. I never touched her again." He looked down at her. "That was a lifetime ago."

Alex heard in her mind his vehemence against ever marrying again, and her heart wanted some reassurance from him that his opinion, his feelings, had changed.

"What about you, Alexandra? How long has it been for you?"

She didn't want to own up to how long it had been, but since she'd started this, she couldn't very well back out now. "My husband was the last man I was intimate with." She didn't mention the doctor she'd dated a couple of years ago. After a few kisses and enduring his groping hands, Alex had ended their relationship.

He chuckled. "We're quite a swinging pair."

His comment made Alex realize they hadn't used any sort of protection. She moaned. "We're so swinging that we didn't use any protection."

"We didn't exactly plan this."

He was right. He hadn't set out to seduce her.

A cough carried on the night air, reminding them that Sarah was in the house.

Alexandra scrambled off the bed, picked up her nightgown and slipped into it. "I need to get back to my room." She shoved her arms into the sleeves of her robe and knotted the belt.

He stood and grasped her head in his hands. "Something special happened here, tonight, Doc."

"I know."

"I don't want to let it go."

"I can't spend the night in your room," she argued.

"I know that. But before you leave me, I want you to know that whatever this is between us, I want to hold on to it for as long as you're here."

The hope in her heart died. He said nothing of her staying here and loving him the rest of their lives. He was only speaking of their sharing their bodies while she was here in Saddle.

"'Night," she mumbled, and raced from the room. Once safely behind the closed door of her bedroom, she felt the crushing weight of despair roll over her and she sank to the floor. This time she couldn't cry. There were no tears left. Only an aching hole.

Derek stumbled back to the bed and sat down. He held his head in his hands and took a deep breath, trying to clear his head so he could think. He'd just experienced the most powerful loving of his life, and he wanted to wrap his arms around Alexandra and tell her he loved her. He wanted to protect her, comfort her, be there for her in the dark hours of the night.

But somehow, something had gone wrong. When he'd tried to tell her he wanted to continue their relationship, hoping that she would give him a sign that she'd be willing to stay out here in this part of Texas, she had backed away from him.

How could she turn away from what they'd shared? And yet, he knew the other forces that pulled at her. Her past with her father, the ugly memories of this past year, and her ambivalent feelings toward her medical practice. Could he ask her to ignore all those issues and stay here in Saddle with him?

If she could come to grips with her past, would she consider staying with him and Sarah?

Was he ready to risk his heart without any guarantees that his love would be returned?

He wrestled with the questions the rest of the night, but he found no answers.

Chapter 11

At eight-thirty the next morning Derek and Alex drove to the clinic and discovered a crowd gathered at the front door, proving Derek's prediction of last night. He dropped off Alexandra, then continued to his office.

As soon as he opened the door, the phone rang. Derek snatched the receiver from its cradle. "Hello."

"How's it going, Derek?" Sheriff Wesley Clayton asked. "DEA turn up any new leads?"

Derek took off his brown cowboy hat and laid it on the desk. "I haven't checked with them this morning. Did you run the license plate on that Chevy we found the other day?"

"The plates were stolen off a car in El Paso. We don't know who owned the Chevy."

"Terrific," Derek grumbled. "Have you heard of anyone in the market for steroids? Maybe we can track it from that direction."

"No. I talked with the coaches at the university and the high school. If anyone is using, it's an isolated case. Nothing widespread. But maybe our smugglers are aiming for a larger city with more gyms and people wanting to bulk up."

Derek sighed. His eyes burned from lack of sleep. Breakfast had been a tense affair, with neither him nor Alex knowing what to say. Thankfully Sarah had filled in the awkward silences.

"Derek, you okay?" Wes asked.

The question snapped Derek back to the present. "Remember I told you that the postmistress was being tested for TB?"

"Yes."

"Well, she's got it. The entire town and probably all the surrounding ranches are going to have to be tested."

"Who's going to do that?"

"Dr. Courtland offered to stay."

"Oh? What happened? What convinced her to stay? Was it your handsome mug?"

Derek wanted to laugh at the ridiculous question, but he couldn't manage it. "A lot of people talked her into it. I'll call out to the ranch and if there's any new information from the DEA guys, I'll let you know."

The next two and a half hours were filled with half a dozen calls from worried citizens. As Derek finished his conversation with the DEA agents, Billy Mayer strolled into his office.

"The doc's car is fixed," he announced, sliding into the chair in front of the desk. "The water pump arrived this morning on the bus. I just finished putting it in."

"I'm sure Alexandra will be thrilled to know she can leave anytime she wants."

Billy sat up straighter. "Alexandra?"

Derek glared at his friend.

"You think she's going to split?"

"You're behind on your gossip, Billy. The doctor is going to stay for a couple of months until we can get someone to manage all the TB cases."

Billy grinned. "Hey, I didn't do such a bad job, did I?"

His friend's meddling had turned Derek's world upside down and inside out. He didn't know whether to smash his fist into Billy's face or congratulate him for bringing Alexandra into their lives. He did neither. Instead, he grabbed his hat and stalked out of his office.

"Where you going?" Billy called out.

"To see the doc and tell her her car is ready. She'll get a real charge out of that."

Alex glanced at the clock for the hundredth time that morning. Eleven. The PPD tests had not arrived and the waiting room was filled with people. The citizens of Saddle had been patient, cooperative and not a word of complaint had passed anyone's lips.

She picked up the phone and called Alpine. Dr. Shelly wasn't in his office and no one knew anything about the PPD tests.

Alex walked out of the office and down to the waiting room. All talk ceased and everyone turned to her. "I tried to contact Dr. Shelly in Alpine. He wasn't in and I couldn't get any information on the status of the PPD tests. Until I can find a supply of these tests, there's no need for you all to wait here. Please call me late this afternoon. I'll let you know what's going on."

As the people filed out, Derek appeared in the doorway. The sight of him made her heart beat faster, and beautiful memories of the night before flooded her brain. He took off his Stetson and ran his fingers through his hair. She knew how silky those strands were. She took a deep, calming breath.

"What's going on?" he asked after the last person departed.

His question was a welcome diversion because it gave her something to talk about besides what had occurred between them. Eventually they would have to discuss their relationship, but for the moment she had a reprieve. Quickly she explained to him about the missing tests.

"What are you going to do?"

Alex's mind raced. There was more than one way to skin a cat. And she wasn't going to be at the mercy of Dr. Shelly anymore. "I'm going to call Houston." She turned and raced back to the office.

"Why Houston?" he asked, trailing behind her.

She punched in the number for Ben Taub Hospital and asked for Everett Carlin.

"Your boss?"

She opened her mouth to respond but Everett came on the line.

"Alex, I hadn't expected to hear from you so soon."

A laugh bubbled out of her mouth. "I'm not calling to ask you to find me a hit man." But the idea had crossed her mind.

"You had me worried for a minute."

She smiled. "What I do need from you are PPD tests."

"I thought you were getting them out of Alpine."

"Those tests haven't shown up and I can't wait. Can you get me a hundred tests and do it today?"

"Alex, you don't ask for small favors, do you?"

"That's why I called you. I knew if anyone could pull it off, it was you."

"You trying to flatter me?"

"Yes."

Everett laughed. "I'll try."

"Call me here at the clinic when you round them up. Then I want you to put those tests on a Southwest Airlines airplane to Midland. I'll have one of my dad's pilots standing by to fly them out to me via helicopter. Also, do you have Zeke's number? I'm going to need INH, ethambutol, pyrazinamide and rifampin. I have a patient who needs medication and I can't wait around on Dr. Shelly."

Everett gave her the number and Alex contacted the representative for the drug company. She quickly arranged for the drugs to be shipped with the tests. As she dialed her father's number, she glanced at Derek. "This is one of the benefits of having a wealthy father."

Alex breathed a sigh of relief that her father wasn't in the office. She explained the situation to his secretary and arranged for the flight from Midland to Saddle. "Thanks, Dolores. If you talk to my mom, tell her I'll come by and see her when I'm finished here."

"You need to call her, *chica*. She misses you."

The old guilt that had plagued her since she left home reared its ugly head. She would have liked to spend more time with her mother, but in order to escape her father's overprotective influence, she had to limit her visits home. "I will." When she hung up, she found Derek studying her.

"It looks like you have some of your father's wheeling-dealing talent."

A blush stained her cheeks, and she lifted one shoulder in a casual gesture. After spending a lifetime observing her dad, some of it had to rub off. "If you think I've got the technique down, you ought to meet my older sister."

"The one in Dallas?"

Alex nodded.

An uncomfortable silence descended between them. His gaze roamed slowly over her, tracing the lines of her face, moving down her neck to sweep over her breasts and belly. Heat followed in the wake of his gaze as if he had physically touched her. His eyes darkened and the sparks of awareness that were always there leaped high.

Alex was the first to look away, fearing if she didn't, she'd rush across the room and throw herself in Derek's arms and beg him to love her again.

He cleared his throat. "I came by to tell you that Billy has your car fixed."

Her first impulse was to laugh hysterically. Now that she was emotionally and physically committed to staying here until a replacement could be found, her car was working again. She stumbled backward toward the desk and sank onto the edge. "I guess that means I can drive myself between this clinic and your house."

He chuckled. "That will put miles on your Mustang."

The shrill ring of the phone filled the room. Alex answered.

"Alex, this is Everett. I got your tests and Zeke will have your medicine ready in a few minutes. The stuff will be on Southwest flight thirty-four. It will arrive in Midland at four forty-five."

"You lived up to your reputation, Everett. Thanks."

"To whom should I submit the bill for the tests?" Everett asked in a deadpan tone. But Alex knew him well enough to know he was teasing. Ev had a heart as big as the state he lived in.

She laughed. "Spoken like the head of a department of a county hospital."

"If you need anything else, let me know."

"Oh, I do need something else. You know those pill dispensers that are labeled Sunday through Saturday? Well, I'll need some of those."

"Alex, I'm not the local discount store. Tell your people to go out and buy them."

"Everett, if I'm going to play doctor, nurse and caretaker for these people, I'm going to need some help. Now, if you want to lend me a public health nurse, I'll be happy to accept."

"Sometimes, Alex, you're too smart for my own good. All right, I'll see what I can do."

"You're a prince, Ev."

He mumbled something that sounded like "shoot."

" 'Bye." Alex couldn't suppress a self-satisfied grin as she turned to face Derek. "Everett got the tests. I knew he could do it. He's affectionately known as the miracle worker. If you need something at the hospital, Ev knows what strings to pull."

He stepped toward her. "When will the tests get here?"

She felt the heat of his body like the pull of a gigantic magnet and had to tilt her chin up to see him. The yearning of her heart urged her to slip her arms around his waist and lean her head on his chest, but she resisted the impulse. Her emotions were already raw enough. She didn't need to grate them again. "Late afternoon. I won't have to announce when they get here. The helicopter will get everyone's attention."

Derek ran the backs of his fingers across her cheek. "Alexandra."

Electricity danced over her skin, making her heart race and longing surge. She closed her eyes to hide her reaction from him. The feel of his lips on hers made her eyelids fly open. A chuckle rumbled in his chest.

"Close your eyes, sweetheart. It's not romantic to stare."

His mouth covered hers again. The emotion rising in her crushed her resistance like a tidal wave after an earthquake. Too much had happened in the past few days, and Derek's touch was the one steady thing in her life. She moaned and wrapped her arms around him. Derek didn't need any further encouragement as he pulled her off the desk. One hand cupped her bottom bringing her hard against his arousal. His other hand threaded through the hair at the back of her head.

"Ah, Doc." He sighed against her ear several minutes later. "It's a crime what you do to me."

As a declaration of love it lacked something. The closeness they had shared last night had touched her with a magic that made her believe love could enter her life again. The fear she now faced was whether Derek would allow love back in *his* life.

His mouth covered hers again, making her questions about their relationship evaporate like morning mist under the bright sunlight.

"Derek," a voice called out. "Derek, you here?"

Derek's lips left hers. He rested his forehead against hers. "Damn, what does he want?"

Before Derek could release her, Billy barged into the office. "Oops."

Dropping his arms to his sides, Derek turned and blocked Billy's view of Alexandra. "You wanted something?"

Although Alex couldn't see Derek's expression, the tone of his voice chilled the room.

"The doc's car is outside, running like a top. I even washed it."

Alex stepped around Derek's towering form. She schooled her features in that no-nonsense expression that she wore in the emergency room. "Thank you."

Billy handed her the keys to her car.

"How's your mother-in-law feeling today?" she asked.

"Not too good. She's anxious about what's happening with the post office. I think she's also wanting to start on that medicine you ordered."

"You tell her that her medicine should arrive this afternoon on an Anderson Oil helicopter. When it does, I'll send it out to your house."

"Got it." He gave Derek a self-satisfied grin.

"You open your mouth, Billy, and I'll personally make sure you need dental work. Do you understand me? What happened in this office had better stay right here."

Billy's expression resembled a pouty little boy who'd been caught stealing cookies out of the cookie jar.

"Billy?"

"Yeah, yeah. I'll keep my mouth shut." He paused at the door. "Oh, I almost forgot. Some guy named Beavins called right after you left your office. Said for you to call him back."

Immediately Derek dialed the number of the ranch. After telling his brother to bring Cathy and himself into town to be tested, he asked for Agent Beavins.

Alex moved around the desk and sat down as Derek talked. A frown wrinkled his forehead. Something must've happened in the investigation with the DEA agents, she surmised.

"You leaving right now?" Derek asked the agent. He reached across the desk and grasped her hand as he listened to the agent's response.

"Yeah, I know where it is. I'm leaving now. Be there in twenty minutes."

"What happened?" Alex asked the instant he was off the phone.

"Agent Beavins thought I might want to come with them. They think they've found the landing field for the airplane."

"Where?"

"A site on the western edge of my land, where it joins with the Moore and Schuller properties."

Suddenly the tremendous amount of pressure Derek was under hit Alex. One of the problems he was facing would be enough to cause an ulcer, but the combination of a TB outbreak and the drug investigation had to be overwhelming.

"Alexandra, we need to talk about what's happening between us."

Alex suddenly knew that if they talked about their relationship it would blow up in their faces. Now wasn't the time for analysis and explanations.

Rising on her tiptoes, she softly kissed his mouth. "Go on. We'll talk later when there's time. Right now, both you and I have jobs to do."

He looked at her uncertainly. "You sure?"

"Positive."

He gave her a proper and thorough kiss, snatched his hat from the desk and left.

Alex bit her lip and choked back the tears. Then, without thinking, she grabbed for the phone. The helicopter pilot in Midland needed to know when the supplies would arrive.

The time for talking didn't come that day or the next. Derek called late in the day to say he was staying at the ranch because the DEA agents were staking out the airfield. After talking to Sarah and making sure she didn't feel neglected, he promised Alex they would talk.

The next day was filled with people straggling through the clinic. Alex's time was consumed with charting these patients, questioning how many people lived with them or on their ranch. When she wasn't filling out charts, figuring how many more needed to be tested, she was trying to calm fears and answer questions. That night she fell asleep on the couch.

When Alex woke alone in her room the next morning, she blushed to realize that Derek must have carried her to bed, undressed her except for her bra and panties, and placed her between the sheets.

A gentle rap on the door drew her attention.

"Yes," she called out.

The door slowly opened and Derek stuck his head inside. "You awake, sleepyhead?"

Alex tucked the sheet under her arms as she sat up. "I guess I was more tired than I thought."

He stepped inside and walked to the bed.

"Thanks for putting me to bed—"

A speculative gleam shone in his eyes as he waited for her to say more.

"I mean—"

"Yes?"

"You did carry me to bed, didn't you?" It was a stupid question. Obviously he was the only one in the house who could've.

"I did." He sat next to her and laced his fingers through hers. "It's almost seventy-two hours since you gave me my TB test."

She glanced down at his forearm covered by the sleeve of his uniform.

"This afternoon Sarah will need her test read."

Alex waited. He wanted to say more.

His thumb stroked over the back of her hand in a soothing manner. He looked into her eyes and she saw his worry. "I'm not concerned for myself," he began. "It's Sarah. I can tell from the way she's fussing in the kitchen that she's nervous."

"I am, too." He seemed startled by her announcement. "Derek, I care for Sarah. No matter how things come out, she's going to weather this storm. And you'll be here for her, and in the long run your love will make the difference in her life."

"Is Sarah the only one you care for?"

His question was like a dagger in her heart. How could he ask that question after what they had shared together? She scanned his face, needing some sign from him. Her first instinct was to retreat from the pain, but the uncertainty lurking in the depths of his eyes pulled at her. Maybe he needed reassurance, too.

Her fingers brushed back the lock of hair resting on his forehead. "No. I'm especially fond of her daddy. He's got the sexiest dimple in his cheek that makes me crazy every time I see it."

He perked up. "Really." The dimple appeared.

Maybe she'd given him a little too much reassurance. Lightly her fingers traced the indentation. "Yeah."

His hand came up and covered hers. "Alexandra—" He stopped himself. Pulling her hand away from his face, he kissed the palm and then released her. "I'd better let you get dressed. I get the odd feeling that today's going to be as crazy as yesterday."

That she didn't doubt.

When she appeared in the kitchen twenty minutes later, showered and in fresh jeans and T-shirt, Alex realized that Derek hadn't understated Sarah's nervousness. The girl was standing by the table, glancing at her arm.

"Good morning," Alex offered cheerfully, hoping to ease the tension in the room.

Sarah's head snapped up. She tried to smile but her bottom lip began to tremble. Alex opened her arms, and Sarah flew into them.

Alex's eyes filled with tears and her heart flooded with love. This child had managed to slip beneath her guard and find a part of her heart that still worked. Alex's gaze locked with Derek's. Her dad had pulled off the same trick. Father and daughter were firmly entrenched.

"I'm scared."

"I know, honey. But there's nothing to worry about. I'm here. Your dad's here."

After a few moments Sarah pulled out of Alex's arms and gave her a watery smile.

Alex smiled back and gently wiped a tear from Sarah's cheek. "Let's eat. Then I'll read your dad's test."

Breakfast was cold cereal and fruit. After the dishes were loaded in the dishwasher, the three sat back down at the table. Alex had a washable marker in her hand.

"All right, Sarah. Let me show you how the test is read." She motioned to Derek. "Deputy," she said in mock severity, "would you please roll up your sleeve."

"Which one?" he asked.

Alex knew he was striving to make this moment light. "The right one."

He unbuttoned his cuff and rolled up the sleeve. Alex took his hand and pulled so his forearm rested on the flat surface of the table. "First I'll draw a line around the reaction area." She traced the edge of the rising. "Then with this metric ruler, I measure the size. Since your dad has been exposed to TB, that puts him in a high-risk group. If the lump is under five millimeters it's considered negative. Over is positive." She placed the ruler by the reaction area. "Four millimeters. It looks like your dad's test is negative."

Sarah flung herself into Derek's arms. "I'm so glad, Daddy," she whispered.

"I am, too, sweetie."

Alex breathed a sigh of relief. If Sarah had TB— which they didn't know at this point—her father wasn't the one who had given it to her.

Derek's gaze met hers and Alex was struck by the thought that it had been the height of stupidity to make love to a man who might have TB. Not only had she not known if Derek had been positive for TB, but they also had not used any form of birth control. As a doctor who treated people for all the diseases they got from unprotected sex, she should've acted with more wisdom.

Unfortunately, she had acted like a woman in love—stupid.

Alex stood. "I'm going to drive my car over to the clinic to let everyone know I'm there. Sarah, you'll need to come over after noontime."

"Okay."

As Alex left the room, she thought she saw Derek mouth the words *I love you* over Sarah's head. She couldn't be sure.

Derek left his office and walked down the alley between the buildings. His backyard was directly behind his office and single jail cell.

Fear clutched at his heart. He had this terrible premonition about Sarah. If the worst came true, he was sure that Alexandra would do her best to help Sarah get well. There wasn't another doctor he would rather have take care of his daughter.

Sarah greeted him at the door, her faced pinched and worried.

He tried to appear confident. "You ready?"

She nodded. "I don't think my test is going to turn out as good as yours." She pushed up her sleeve and Derek saw the swelling on the inside of her forearm.

He took her hand. "However it turns out, sweetie, we're going to get through this together."

Her tearful expression cut through his heart.

"Remember what Alexandra told you the other day, about your guardian angel guiding her here? Well, I have to agree with her. I think we've got the best doctor in the state."

She thought a moment. "I think you're right, Daddy."

"I know I am."

Sarah and Derek showed up, hand in hand, a little after noon.

"Hi, guys," Alex said, trying to appear casual. She was nervous about Sarah's test results.

"How's it gone this morning?" Derek asked, trying to appear calm, but she knew from the strained look in his eyes that he, too, was concerned.

"Busy. Billy has active TB. Lorraine's is inactive."

"Inactive?" Sarah's brow wrinkled in a frown.

Alex sat in one of the chairs in the waiting room and patted the one next to her. Sarah joined her.

"Let me see if I can explain this. Lorraine had been exposed to the TB germs since she lives with Norma and has the bacteria in her body. But her body's defenses are working, protecting her from getting sick. So even though Lorraine's carrying the germ, she can't give it to anyone." Alex drew a deep breath. "If I don't treat her, she could carry the germ in her body the rest of her life and not get sick. Or, at some point in the future, her body's defenses could become weak, the TB germ could flourish and she'd get active TB. For that reason, I'm going to put her on medication."

Derek and Sarah were quiet. Alex stood. "C'mon back to the examining room."

A few minutes later Alex studied Sarah's arm with a sinking heart. Six millimeters. She glanced up into the worried expressions of both father and daughter. "You're at six."

Sarah's face tightened.

"Let's take an X ray."

After developing the film, Alex put it on the viewer.

"How does it look?" Derek asked over her shoulder.

There was a small spot on the right lung. Sarah had only recently contracted the disease. Alex couldn't prevent the smile breaking out on her face. She turned to the others. "It's good news. Although Sarah has active TB, it's in the beginning stages. I'm going to get her on medication, and I see no reason why she won't be one hundred percent cured within a year."

Alex watched the girl's expression carefully, gauging Sarah's reaction. A positive attitude was an important ingredient in getting well. The girl's struggle showed plainly on her face. First fear, then doubt, then a spark of hopefulness.

Alex clasped Sarah's shoulders. "Do you believe me? Do you trust me to do everything I can as a doctor to help you get well?"

The little spark flared. "Yes."

The trust Sarah had just handed Alex healed another part of her broken heart. And for the first time in a very, very long time Alex was glad she was a doctor. "All right, sweetie, we're going to do this together. I'm going to get your medication, and I want you to take those pills before you leave the clinic. Let's weigh you.''

"Why?" Sarah asked, stepping onto the scale.

"Because of your age, I have to base the amount of your medication on your weight.''

After Alex took Sarah's weight and figured the dosage, she gave Sarah her medication.

"Are you going to get sick?" Sarah asked after swallowing the last pill.

Alex took Sarah's hand and squeezed it. "Thank you for being concerned, but I've worked with other people who have had TB and not gotten sick. But people like me who work with infectious patients are tested often. Before I leave, I'll test myself." She turned to Derek. A muscle in his jaw flexed and his gaze bored into hers. Alex had the feeling he was annoyed at her for some reason. "You'll have to notify the school about Sarah. And I think until we know the situation, it would be best if they canceled school for the next few days."

"Would it be easier if you went there this afternoon and did all the tests at the same time?" Derek asked.

"You've got a point."

"I'll take you over after I check with the sheriff and get an update on things."

"All right. Also, I'm going to need for you to sit down with me in a day or so and look over the list of people I've tested and let me know if we're missing anyone."

He nodded. "It seems you've got your job cut out for you."

"It should be better in a couple of days once I get a handle on things."

"I hope so, Alexandra. I really hope you're right."

Derek turned off the kitchen light and walked into the living room. He saw Alex close her eyes and lean her head back against the cushions of the sofa.

"Tired?"

"Yeah."

"Roll your head forward."

She obeyed. Her hair parted like a curtain revealing the delicate white skin at the base of her neck. The sight hit him like a fist in the gut, and he wanted to kiss that tender spot. Alex moaned in delight as his fingers worked the tension out of her shoulders.

He felt he was caught in the violent winds of a tornado. Everything around him was moving and shifting with a speed that made his head spin.

In the midst of this confusion there was a growing center of calm—his feelings for Alexandra. He loved her. After the night of passion they had shared, he'd had little doubt of his feelings. And he knew from Alex's response to him that she definitely felt a passion for him.

But what had made his love for Alex absolutely dead-on right was the moment she had held Sarah in her arms this morning.

The one critical point in this relationship that worried Derek was to what degree Alexandra cared for him and Sarah. Did she care enough to commit her life to them and stay here in Saddle?

"You've put in a lot of hours over the past few days," he said, trying to think of a way to draw out her feelings.

"So have you. Has anything turned up out at the airfield?"

"Not a thing. It might be another three weeks before whoever is smuggling decides he needs another load of drugs. That's why I had to drive to Alpine this afternoon. The sheriff's department and DEA wanted to plan how to handle the rest of this investigation."

Derek felt her body relax under the warmth of his hands. But as the tension drained out of her muscles, another kind of tenseness replaced it. "What are you going to do?" she asked.

"Give it a month. If we can't catch them in that time, then we'll junk the surveillance." His fingers ran up into her scalp, causing shivers to dance down her spine. "I'm sorry I couldn't go with you to the school today."

"It wasn't your fault. You had your job to do."

He grunted. "Is that the list of who you've tested so far?"

"Yes."

He moved around the couch and sat beside her. Taking the yellow tablet from her hands, he surveyed the list.

"Good night, Dad, Alex," Sarah said, coming into the room.

Derek set aside the tablet, opened his arms and gave Sarah a big hug. He placed a kiss on the top of her head, and his actions went straight to Alex's heart. How could she shield herself from a man who so tenderly kissed his daughter good-night?

She couldn't and there was no use lying to herself.

Sarah paused in front of Alex. " 'Night."

Alex caught Sarah's hand, pulled her close and hugged her. "Sweet dreams." Her voice brimmed with emotion.

Sarah smiled shyly, then left the room.

At that moment, watching Alex give Sarah the love she'd never had from her mother, Derek decided he'd fight for Alexandra's love. No matter what it took.

"Thank you," Derek whispered. He tucked a strand of hair behind her ear.

Her gaze dropped to her hands, resting in her lap. "There's nothing to thank me for."

His fingers stroked down the side of her neck. "But there is. You forget that all the love and care Sarah's known at the hands of a woman comes from my ex-wife and it isn't much."

Derek silently cursed his stupid remark about his ex-wife. He didn't want to remind her of his failed marriage.

"With this TB outbreak, Sarah needs more than I could give her. I don't know what I would've done if you hadn't been here."

She shrugged. He leaned closer and kissed the soft skin behind her ear.

She turned her head, obviously prepared to tell him now was not the time for this. Her lips grazed his. Framing her head between his hands, he lightly traced the outline of her bottom lip with the tip of his tongue. Her gaze flew to his and he read her passion and need.

His mouth sipped from hers, finally coaxing from her a moan. He deepened the kiss, his tongue tangling with hers.

In the small part of his brain that still functioned he heard a door close and realized that Sarah was still awake. Alex must've heard it too, because she jerked away from him.

"We'd better look over that list."

As he glanced at the tablet behind him on the cushion, Derek realized that Alex was trying to slide out of this emotional encounter the way she did other emotional issues in her life. She was hiding from it. Well, he wasn't going to let her. "Alexandra?"

"What?" she answered, avoiding looking into his face.

His fingers captured her chin, bringing her gaze to his. "Come to me later tonight. I need you, and I think you need me." He held his breath. It was a gamble to issue the invitation, but he didn't know any other way to make her choose.

"I—"

"For once, sweetheart, give in to your heart."

Chapter 12

As Alexandra lay alone in her bed several hours later, Derek's words continued to play over in her head, again and again and again.

He was wrong, she thought crossly. She'd given in to her heart many times. She could name several examples: med school was one, falling in love with Vince was another. Even her service with the Red Cross had come from her heart. It certainly hadn't come from an instinct of self-preservation.

And yet, if she was honest with herself, she'd have to admit those instances were actually a reaction to something. Her choice of career had been fashioned by her younger sister's accident, but her marriage to Vince had been a heart matter.

Was it really? a traitorous little voice in her head asked. If she compared her feelings for Derek against those she'd had for Vince, her feelings for Vince were a pale echo.

She stilled.

Another ugly and treacherous thought occurred. If Vince had lived, they would've probably divorced. She and Vince had had nothing in common except medicine. Vince hadn't understood about her convoluted relationship with her father, or her passion to escape west Texas. He wasn't comfortable with horses or cowboys, and despite being born in Texas, he'd never understood why his fellow Texans gloried in their past. But the most crucial point was that, although he'd been a thoughtful lover, he'd never created in her the depth of passion that Derek did.

And since she was being painfully honest with herself, she might as well admit her real motive for going to Bosnia. Yes, she had wanted to help those people, but in helping others, it was the best way to ignore the loneliness in her own life. If she was busy with other people's problems, she wouldn't have time to deal with her own.

This time, though, her heart demanded to be heard, and she couldn't ignore it. What she had with Derek was precious, something that needed to be nourished and fed.

But if she gave in to her heart's demands, and things didn't work out, what then? Could she live through that final, crippling blow? If she didn't give in to her heart's demands, would she ever be a whole person again?

She remembered Derek's kissing Sarah good-night, then recalled his fierce tenderness when he had touched her and made love to her several nights ago.

Was it worth the risk? Yes, it was.

Alex threw back the covers and pulled on her robe. Swallowing her rising nervousness, she slipped out of her room and walked the half-dozen steps down the hall to Derek's room. By natural measure, the distance was only several feet, but for Alexandra, those steps represented the longest journey of her life.

Her fingers shook as she turned the brass knob and pushed open the door.

Moonlight streamed through the open curtains, giving the room a pearly glow, and making Alex wonder if she was dreaming.

"I'm glad you came."

Alex's gaze flew to the bed. The opalescent moonlight fell across the lower part, and she saw Derek's legs outlined under the covers. His face and upper body were in the shadows.

"I was worried you wouldn't."

She squinted and saw that he was sitting up, a pillow propped behind his back.

"I—" She fell silent. Nothing appropriate came to mind. She didn't want to admit the argument she'd had with herself.

"Are you going to stay by the door all night?" There was a lightness in his voice that eased her nervousness. She started toward him, but then stopped. She had come this far, but she needed him to meet her. She'd given in to her heart. Now it was time for him to do the same.

"Yeah, I think so."

He leaned forward, bringing his face into the light. His elbows rested on his knees, his hands clasped together. His brow wrinkled as he studied her. After a moment his sexy grin split his face. "If you want to make love standing up, Doc, I'm more than willing to accommodate you."

Before she could sputter a protest, he threw back the covers and was striding toward her, every inch of his glorious nude frame outlined by the light. Logical thought fled her brain as she was enveloped in his strong arms and hauled up off the floor and against his chest. The only thought she had was that she had come home.

When his mouth came crushing down on hers, she welcomed his fierceness. It matched the need in her. She felt the solid wood of the door behind her back as he whispered in her ear, "Put your legs around my waist."

She looked into his eyes. "You can't be serious?"

That grin appeared again. "Can't I? Put your legs around my waist, Alexandra. Let me show you how it can be between us."

The intensity of his words rocked her. She obeyed, compelled to experience the promise in his eyes. His fingers tugged her gown and robe out of the way and then she felt him slide home. She moaned and her head rolled back against the door.

"Feel that, sweetheart. We're one."

The truth of his words sang through her veins.

"Look at me, Alexandra. I want to see your eyes go dark with passion when you touch heaven with me."

Her eyes fluttered open and locked with his. Their souls were one as surely as their bodies.

As they moved together and plunged into ecstasy, Alex knew that her heart had been right.

Later Derek held Alex while she slept, and he allowed himself to believe that maybe there was a future for them. As he had lain in bed waiting for her, he'd prayed she would listen to her heart. When she finally slipped into his room, it had taken him several moments to realize that she wasn't a figment of his wishful imagination.

He frowned as he remembered her refusal to walk across the room to his bed. Had she been trying to tell him something important and he missed it? Tonight she had yielded to her heart, but would she tomorrow? And what about the day after that?

If he had anything to say about it, she would. Whatever had bothered her, he was determined to discover it and deal with it.

After their incredible lovemaking, he wanted to whisper in her ear that he loved her and intended to marry her, but he feared it was too early to press that issue.

He was gambling that, over the next month or so, the bonds they were building both inside the bedroom and out would be so strong that she would never want to leave him. He would hold her here with bonds of passion and friendship.

Yes, it was a gamble. But he'd just won the first hand.

Alex studied the scribbling before her, charting the percentage of TB cases within family groups. Norma was at the center of the chart. Her family had had fifty percent of the individuals with active TB.

The next circle, like concentric rings in a pool, was the co-workers and friends of Norma, Billy and Lorraine. For each of those individuals who tested positive, their family group would have to be tested. Any family group that had a percentage of positive results above thirty percent had to be suspected as the source of this outbreak.

"What are you doing?"

Alex looked up from the desk to see Derek standing in the doorway to the clinic office. She ruffled the papers before her. "Trying to figure out who our ground zero patient is in all this mess."

He strolled around the desk and lightly kissed the particularly sensitive spot on the side of her neck that he'd found last night. Shivers skated over her skin.

"Stop that," she admonished him. "We don't know who will walk in."

He wagged his brows and gave her a sensual, knowing smile.

"How many people can you threaten to punch, aside from Billy, and be sure they won't talk?"

He folded his arms across his chest and leaned back against the desk. "Would it be so bad if people knew about us?"

And what would people say? The doc is sleeping with the deputy. Alex didn't like the sound of that. Call her Victorian, but being named a man's lover didn't set well with her. "Do you want Sarah to know about us?"

His gaze remained steady as he studied her. After a long silence he opened his mouth, then closed it. He nodded toward the chart on her desk. "Do you want me to look over your list to see if we've missed anyone?"

"Yes."

He pushed away from the desk. Looking over her shoulder, he scanned her chart. Alex pulled the list of patients she had tested thus far. "Here's the list of who's been in, but I don't have all the results of those tests yet." Her finger ran down the column by the names. "I have five people coming in today for results, and seven tomorrow."

He rubbed his hand over his chin.

"Am I missing any major group of people? Are all the ranches represented?"

"No. I don't see anyone from the Moore ranch. Also, the Davis ranch. I don't see anyone on the list from there."

"Do members of these two ranches come into town to get their mail?"

He placed his mouth next to her ear. "That's the only way they get their mail, Doc."

"Okay." She knew she'd asked a stupid question. "I'll need to call both ranches and have the contact person come into town." She glanced up at him and found his mouth less than an inch from hers.

"I dare you," he whispered.

There was something in the challenge that Alex couldn't resist and her mouth met his. A little imp inside made her want to rock Mr. Deputy Sheriff back on his heels. Her tongue ran over the seam of his lips, then slipped inside when he opened to her. Her hands ran over his shoulders then up into the hair at the back of his head.

A growl rumbled in Derek's chest and he pulled her to her feet.

"Hello." A voice drifted down the hall. "Anyone here?"

They broke away from each other.

Derek cursed. "It's not easy trying to romance a doctor," he muttered.

Alex bit back a smile. "It comes with the territory."

"Hello," the voice called again.

"Back here," Derek shouted back.

A tall man in his early forties appeared. He looked at Derek and nodded. "Derek."

"Hi, Marv. The doc and I were just discussing you."

"Oh?"

Derek turned to Alex. "Alexandra, you won't have to make one of those calls this afternoon. This is Marvin Davis."

"Fred over at the feed store told me to come over here and get tested for TB. What's going on?"

"Sit down, Marv, and Dr. Courtland and I will explain it to you."

"Okay, Beavins, I'll think of a way." Derek glanced up when he heard a noise. Alex stood just inside the doorway of his office watching him talk on the phone. "I'll talk to you tomorrow." He hung up. "What can I do for you, Doc?"

"I thought I'd come by and tell you that your brother and sister-in-law had negative results. Both are well."

He breathed a sigh of relief.

She walked to the desk. "I also got hold of Simon Moore. He said he'd try to wander in sometime in the next few days." She grinned. "I told him to make it as soon as possible."

"That's it," Derek said, jumping to his feet. "You're brilliant, Alexandra." He kissed her cheek.

She frowned and looked at him as if he'd lost his marbles. "Care to tell me what you consider brilliant?"

"Why don't you sit down?"

She took the chair in front of the desk. He sat on the corner of the desk.

"Remember when the DEA agents discovered the airfield?" She nodded. "It borders three ranches. Mine and my brother's, the Schullers' and the Moore ranch. Now we've eliminated my ranch as one of the suspects. Stan Schuller is in his seventies and there's no reason to suspect him of smuggling. That leaves the Moore ranch. Beavins wanted me to think of a way to get on the ranch without Simon Moore becoming suspicious."

"Is he a suspect?" she asked.

"Not officially. But since the landing strip is situated between the ranches, the logical step is to check out the owners to see if any are involved with the smuggling."

"How does that tie in with me?"

"The TB testing. I can drive you out this afternoon and you test everyone there. We'll use the excuse that because of the public health concern, you couldn't wait for Simon to wander in. Isn't that right?"

She pursed her lips. "That's right."

He squatted on his haunches before her. "I can tell from your expression that you weren't too thrilled with Simon's response. This would be a way to get the testing out of the way, and—" he leaned forward and whispered in her ear "—get back at him." His lips caressed the lobe of her ear.

She jerked her head back and glared at him.

"I'm right, aren't I?"

After a moment her expression softened and her lips twitched. She bit her bottom lip to stop the movement. "When did you want to go?"

"How about now?"

"Don't you want to say hello to your brother and his wife? They're at the feed store getting their mail."

"I'll go by and ask them to stay with Sarah until we get back from the Moore place. You go to the clinic and get several tests. I think there are four people at Simon's ranch, but he might have more help since I was out there the last time." He paused. "So how about it, Doc? You want to go?"

"I'll meet you at the clinic in five minutes."

She started to rise, but he reached out and cupped her chin. "You know what, Alexandra?"

"What?"

"Excuse me." Todd Grey's familiar voice interrupted from the doorway.

Derek released Alex's chin, closed his eyes and let his head roll forward.

He felt Alex slip out of the chair. "I'll see you in five minutes," she said as she left his office.

"Did I interrupt something?" Todd asked.

Derek stood. "No, brother. Alexandra and I were just talking about you."

"Oh? What were you saying lip to lip?"

With a sigh of resignation that Alex had again slipped away before he could tell her how he felt, Derek explained the situation to his brother. It occurred to him a few minutes later, as Alex climbed into his Jeep, that maybe she still wasn't ready to hear what was in his heart.

He hoped she reached that point real soon.

Alex stared out at the rugged horizon. The volcanic mountains in the distance looked as if someone had taken an old-time can opener and cut jagged peaks from a huge mass of rock. An unexpected shower had dumped just enough rain on the area to make the dirt roads messy. But the rain had also filled the air with a refreshing herbal smell.

"What's that I'm smelling?" she asked.

"What?" Derek glanced at her.

"That wonderful smell that the rain brought with it. What is it?"

He took a couple of sniffs. "Oh, that. It's greasewood."

Alex chuckled. "What an awful name for such a wonderful-smelling plant."

He shrugged. "I can't help what it's named."

Alex closed her eyes and breathed in the comforting smell. A comforting smell? Her eyes popped open and she stared at the landscape before her. She searched her heart for a negative feeling or reaction. There wasn't any. Instead, what she discovered was a soft peace.

"Oh, dear Lord," she murmured.

"Are you talking to the Almighty, Doc?"

She turned on the seat to face Derek. "As a matter of fact, Deputy, I am."

"What are you saying?"

"Thank you for a miracle."

He waited for an explanation.

"I *see* this land," she explained, awe in her voice. "I think I know what you see in it."

He grabbed her hand, brought it up to his lips and kissed it. "That is a miracle."

She laughed, a feeling of freedom welling up in her soul.

"Believe me, Doc, I plan to thank the Almighty myself."

* * *

The Jeep's right front wheel fell into a large hole in the road.

"Simon needs to get this road fixed," Derek grumbled, trying to avoid biting his tongue on the jarring ride.

The barn came into view.

"It looks like Mr. Moore needs to paint his barn, too," Alexandra muttered.

Derek glanced at the cracked, peeling white paint on the structure. Several of the side boards were broken off near the ground and needed to be replaced. Derek wondered how Simon could care so little for his livestock to allow that to happen.

The road curved around the barn, bringing the main house into view. Parked in the circular driveway at the front of the house was a new black Cadillac. Derek stopped his Jeep behind the other car and turned off the engine.

"It's a nice car." Alex nodded to the auto in front of them. "If it belonged to me, I'd pave my road to keep the suspension in alignment."

Derek glanced at Alex. "You're an unusual woman, Alexandra Courtland."

"Why, because I worry about the suspension of a car?" she asked as she climbed out. In her hand she carried her little black doctor's bag.

"Because few people would be thoughtful enough to worry about that." Walking between the vehicles, he glanced at the wheels of the Cadillac, looking at the tread of the tires to see if they might resemble any of the distinct tread marks at the airfield.

"What are you doing?"

He shook his head. "Later," he murmured. He lifted the brass knocker and rapped it several times. The sound echoed through the house. After he knocked a second time, the door opened.

"Yeah?" a burly man demanded, his voice low and raspy. He was dressed in a black T-shirt pulled tight across his massive chest. The short sleeves of the shirt cut into the hard muscle of his biceps. The veins of his arms stood out, the muscle so hard it forced the vessels toward the surface. But in spite of his muscle-bound appearance, the guy appeared flushed and his eyes glassy.

Alex glanced at Derek, then at the man at the door.

"You need something?" the man questioned, hostility ringing in his words. The deep roughness of the man's voice, a result of thickened vocal cords, was a dead giveaway that the guy was on massive dosages of steroids.

Not caring for the man's attitude, Derek gave the jerk his most chilling look. Alex stepped in front of him, putting herself between him and the hulk.

"I'm Dr. Alexandra Courtland. I talked with Simon Moore earlier today about testing him for TB." The man hesitated. "Would you please inform him we're here?" Alexandra's voice didn't brook any defiance.

Derek had to bite back a smile at the picture they made. Five-foot-five, one-hundred-and-five-pound female bringing to heel the six-foot-two, two-hundred-and-fifty-pound male with a firm tone and a steely look in her eyes.

The man nodded and reluctantly opened the door for them. He led them down a short hall to the living room. "Wait here. I'll get Mr. Moore."

"Thank you." Alex set her bag on the couch.

Derek scanned the room. A new large-screen television stood against one wall. On the opposite wall was an expensive sound system, with CD player and high-quality speakers. Derek found it odd that Simon would have this new equipment, yet let his barn go to hell.

When he looked back at Alexandra, he saw that she was staring at the open doorway, a frown on her face.

"Are you wondering about Simon's friend?" he softly asked.

"I suspect—"

"Steroid abuse?" Derek finished the thought for her.

"Yes. And the danger—" She broke off when they heard footsteps in the hall.

A tall, slender man entered the room. He was dressed in a flowing white shirt, navy slacks and expensive loafers with tassels. Derek wasn't impressed with Simon's attempt at suave, but then again, he was never much impressed with Simon. The man always wanted the good things in life and didn't much care to work for them. Damn, why hadn't it occurred to him earlier about Simon's weakness? He could only attribute his absent-mindedness to the outbreak of TB that had afflicted his friends, neighbors and child.

"Derek, it's good to see you. And this must be Dr. Courtland." Simon Moore shook her hand. "I understand from Randy that you are here to test me for TB. I thought we agreed that I would come into Saddle in the next week." He sounded somewhat put out.

"We did, but since I am trying to pin down the source of this outbreak, I need to test everyone as quickly as I can. Derek was kind enough to volunteer to drive me out here.''

''That was generous of him.'' Simon's tone didn't match his words.

''In addition to you, I'll need to test everyone on the ranch, Randy included.''

The sound of a car engine filtered into the room. Derek walked to the window and watched the Cadillac drive away. From his vantage point Derek couldn't see who was driving. ''Who was in the car?''

''Randy. I had a couple of business errands that needed to be done and he volunteered to do them for me.'' He turned to Alex. ''I'm sorry, Dr. Courtland, I didn't know you wanted to test everyone.''

''When he returns, have him come into Saddle. Today.'' Her last word rang with steel.

''I don't know if he'll be back today.''

The more Simon talked, the more he gave away.

''Whenever he returns, he needs to come immediately to the clinic.'' She glanced around the room. ''I'll need a table. Could we go into the kitchen or dining room?''

Simon led them into the kitchen and introduced them to Mrs. Burns, who was at the stove, stirring what appeared to be a pot of soup.

''If you'll sit down and roll up your sleeve,'' Alex instructed Simon.

''So, doctor, how do you think this TB thing started?'' Simon tried to sound casual, but tension showed in the pinched expression around his eyes.

Alex slipped the needle under his skin and injected the protein. Simon winced and looked away.

''That's what I'm trying to discover, Mr. Moore.''

"Please, call me Simon. How does one get tuberculosis?"

"From prolonged exposure to an individual who has it. The risk goes up if you're in a small enclosed area with the infected person. The post office had to be closed because of those very reasons."

"I see."

"Everyone I test will need to come into Saddle in seventy-two hours to have the results read. I'll start with Mrs. Burns while you round up the rest of your people."

"What were you trying to tell me earlier in the living room when Simon walked in?" Derek asked Alex on their drive back into Saddle.

She thought for a moment, then understanding dawned in her eyes. "Ah, you mean my statement about Randy. Well, if he is a steroid abuser, and I think he is from the deepness of his voice, his muscle mass and his charming greeting—" she gave him a saucy grin and Derek knew she was being sarcastic "—and he catches TB, he's at greater risk than you or I." Her tone sobered. "He could die within weeks of contracting the disease."

"You think he might have TB?"

"I have a bad feeling about him. And although Randy didn't cough in our presence, he did seem flushed."

"And his eyes had that glassy look Sarah gets when she's running a fever."

She folded her arms under her breasts and slid deeper into the seat cushions. "I just hope things aren't too far gone for him."

Derek nodded and stared out at the road. So now there was the prospect of this steroid abuser having a fatal case of TB. That situation could cause a panic throughout the county.

Derek cursed. Damn. What a stupid SOB Simon was.

He shook his head. Everyone in this part of the county knew that after the death of Simon's father, the Moore ranch had gone to hell. Simon had no interest in ranching and less skill. Derek recalled a rumor he'd heard when he first came back to Saddle that the Moore ranch was on the edge of bankruptcy. So how did Simon afford a new car and all that new equipment in his living room? And where had he picked up his newest ranch hand? Randy didn't look as if he knew one end of a horse from the other.

Well, if Derek didn't miss his guess, Simon was involved in the smuggling operation. He'd call Beavins about what he'd discovered once they got back into town.

"Hot damn," Beavins said. "That's terrific news. Do you think we can get a tread match on the Caddy for those at the landing strip?"

"Might. Simon's crony is supposed to come into town today. I could take a print then." Derek carried the phone to his office window and looked at the clinic. Alexandra's Mustang was parked outside along with a red Ford pickup he recognized as belonging to the Douglas ranch. "Also, I think the D.A. would give us a writ to pull the phone records for Simon's ranch. We could see who he's been calling and then run the numbers through the National Crime Information Computer. See if he's been calling any known felons." He watched Maria and Bob Douglas climb into their truck. Derek turned and walked back to his desk. "We might even luck out and find calls to the Mexican pharmaceutical company that manufactured the steroids we picked up."

"I agree," Beavins responded. "I'll talk to my boss in Marfa and suggest it. I'll call you back and let you know what's going on."

At nine o'clock that night Derek and Alex were at the kitchen table charting the results of the day's TB tests when the phone rang.

"Hello," Derek greeted the caller.

"Derek, this is Beavins. We got the writ and are now in the process of checking out the numbers. Did your suspect ever come into town?"

"No, the guy never showed."

"Now, why am I not surprised? I'll call if we turn up anything," Beavins said before hanging up.

Derek joined Alex at the table.

"Who was that?" she asked.

After he explained what was happening, Alex asked incredulously, "You think Simon would be stupid enough to call the Mexican pharmaceutical company?"

Derek leaned over and brushed a kiss across her mouth. "Doc, you wouldn't believe how stupid criminals can be. It's incredible."

Alex snuggled closer to the warmth of Derek's body, reveling in the afterglow of their lovemaking. It amazed her that she had turned out to be such a sensual person. But that aspect of her personality had been brought to life by the handsome man in whose arms she was sheltered.

The bedside clock indicated that dawn was only a few minutes away. Alex turned and kissed Derek on the cheek.

"I like that," he mumbled sleepily.

Her fingers sifted through his hair. "I've got to get back to my room."

His eyes opened and his gaze searched hers. The look in his eyes worried her. He was holding back something that was of great importance to him, something he felt he couldn't share with her.

A chill settled around her heart, and suddenly she didn't want to know Derek's thoughts. She wiggled out of his embrace and slipped on her nightgown and robe. With her hand on the doorknob, she glanced over her shoulder. "See you at breakfast."

He nodded.

Alex raced to her room and climbed into bed. Burying her face in the pillow, she tried to calm her racing heart. What had Derek been holding back?

Don't borrow trouble. The thought drifted through her brain.

Alex tried to logically evaluate the situation, setting aside her feelings. The events around her were rushing to a final climax. The possibilities for the identity of the ground-zero TB patient—the source of the outbreak—were getting narrow. Derek's investigation of the illegal drug smuggling was reaching a critical mass and Alex had the feeling the smuggling was linked to the outbreak of TB. Things seemed confusing and ready to explode. Yet in the midst of this confusion, she had found a small measure of peace.

Some of this calm flowed from making peace with the land—she belonged to it, it was home. The other part came from Derek and Sarah—they had found the portions of her heart that were intact. Because she had something to hold on to, maybe now she could face the rest of the demons that haunted her.

Alex rolled onto her back, the pillow clutched to her chest. Even if Derek didn't want her to stay forever, maybe by the time he asked her to go she would be healed enough to survive walking away.

Maybe.

Chapter 13

Derek looked at Alexandra over the rim of his coffee cup. For the past two days she had behaved strangely.... Maybe strangely wasn't the right word. It was hard for him to put a name to the odd way she was acting. A part of her had somehow withdrawn from him and he didn't know why. He was tempted to tell her how he felt but he was scared that his honesty would drive her farther away, so he kept quiet.

"How are you feeling?" Alex asked Sarah.

Sarah glanced up from her oatmeal. "Okay. But I miss seeing my friends at school."

"Well, I think you can go back next week."

Derek picked up his coffee mug. "Have you narrowed down where the TB outbreak might have started?" he asked Alex.

"Yes. So far, only Norma's family and the Davis family have had TB results over thirty percent. But I think that when I have the results from the Moore ranch, they'll be added to my list of suspects. I plan to drive out to the Davis ranch this morning and interview them, see if I can pinpoint where they were exposed to the bacteria."

"Do you know how to get there?" Sarah asked.

Alex smiled. "I got directions from Mrs. Davis yesterday." She sipped her coffee, then looked at Derek. "What do you plan to do today?"

Derek's heart thumped in his chest. This little exchange seemed right and natural. He, Sarah and Alexandra together, sharing breakfast, was the way it should be. So why couldn't Alexandra see it?

"I'm going out to the ranch. Beavins and I are going to go over some information we've come up with." He didn't want to mention the telephone records in front of his daughter. She didn't need to know his ugly suspicion of Simon Moore. She knew Simon and had often talked to him when he came into the post office for his mail. "Alexandra, I want you to take my mobile phone with you."

A militant light entered her eyes. "Why?"

"Because, if you have any trouble, you can call. It's only for your safety."

Her gaze softened. "What if you need it?"

"I have my police radio. Besides, I know these roads like the back of my hand. If anything happens, I would know where the closest help was."

She nodded. "All right."

Derek stood, and set his cup and bowl in the sink. He kissed Sarah on the cheek, then stopped by Alex's chair and did the same thing. "It's your turn to do the dishes."

She looked up at him, her eyes wide, her mouth hanging open.

"See you later, ladies."

He heard Alex sputter as he walked away.

As Alex unlocked the clinic door she still felt the blush that had stained her face when Derek had kissed her in front of Sarah. Apparently Sarah hadn't shared her embarrassment. In fact, from her reaction, Alex would guess she approved.

Alex walked down the hall to her office and turned on the light. *Her office*. The thought resounded through her head like a cannon shot. Her fingers shook as she picked up the files for the Davis ranch. She was beginning to think of this place as home. And as hard as she tried to guard her heart, she grew more and more involved with these people and this land every day.

She was reaching for the light switch when the front door of the clinic slammed open.

"Help," a male voice yelled.

Alex rushed into the waiting room and found Simon Moore holding up his cohort, Randy. The larger male was sweating, his face flushed with fever. He coughed, and the muscle spasm doubled him over.

Alex recognized the deep, rumbling cough. Snatching a tissue from the box on the coffee table, she handed it to Randy just in time for him to catch the blood he coughed up.

Simon looked away in disgust.

"Help me get him into the examining room," Alex ordered Simon as she set down the files in her hand.

She grabbed one of Randy's arms and Simon took the other as they guided him into the small room.

"How long have you been feeling bad, Randy?" Alex asked. She slipped a thermometer into his mouth.

"A while," he mumbled around the glass tube. "Thought it was the flu."

She took his blood pressure and examined the glands in his throat. Removing the thermometer, she read his temperature. One hundred and three.

"Tell me your symptoms," Alex commanded.

"I feel like hell. Achy, chills, tired, lost weight." His speech was slurred.

"Can you be more specific about how long you've been feeling bad?"

He rubbed his forehead. "Started feeling this way about the time we were in Mexico City with Jorge." He looked at Simon. "How long ago was that?"

Simon nearly choked at Randy's question. For several tense moments the two men glared at each other. Alex didn't doubt that if Simon had had a gun, he would've shot Randy to shut him up.

"How long, Simon?" Randy crossly demanded.

Hostility gleamed in Simon's eyes. "A month."

"Rats," Alex mumbled to herself. "Randy, I need for you to be honest with me. Your life may depend on it." She had his attention now. "How long have you been using steroids?"

Randy shook his head. "Don't know what you're talking about."

Alex placed herself squarely in front of her patient. "There's TB in Saddle. You're exhibiting signs of the disease. If you've been abusing steroids that makes you a high-risk patient and you could easily die from the TB. I can't help you unless I know what I'm dealing with. How long have you been using steroids?"

His gaze touched Simon, then came back to rest on her face. "A year." He coughed again and brought up more blood.

"You need to be hospitalized—now." She walked into her office and phoned the hospital in Alpine. "I have an emergency here. Is the Medi-Vac helicopter available?"

"Yes," the nurse answered.

"I need it dispatched to Saddle. Immediately. I've got a TB patient who's a steroid abuser. I think he's in serious trouble. Warn your doctors."

"The copter will be there in thirteen minutes."

She hung up and walked back into the examining room to speak to Randy. "You're going to the hospital. They can take better care of you there." Alex turned to Simon. "Let's read your TB test."

Simon's expression resembled a thundercloud. His mood darkened further over the next few minutes as she read his test as positive, then took an X ray.

"Am I going to die like Randy?" Simon asked, a rising note of panic in his voice.

Alex glanced away from the film. "Are you abusing like Randy?"

"Do I look bulked up?" The rage rumbling around inside Simon shone in his eyes and the tightness of his jaw.

"What I meant was unless you have some hidden problem I don't know about at this moment—"

The sound of a helicopter broke into her concentration. Alex hurried outside and waved to the chopper hovering overhead. It took less than five minutes to load Randy into the helicopter and give the nurse his vital signs, but by the time Alex finished answering the questions of the gathered crowd and returned to the clinic to speak to Simon, he was gone.

Retrieving the Davises' file from the waiting room, Alex locked the clinic and climbed into her car.

* * *

"Hi, sweetie, how are things going there at home?" Derek asked Sarah, shifting the phone from one ear to the other. He and Beavins had spent the past hour closeted in the ranch office going over Simon's phone records.

"You missed all the excitement, Dad. Some guy who works for Mr. Moore got sick, and Alex got a helicopter to take him to Alpine."

A sense of doom settled over his heart. "Did Alex go with the guy to Alpine?"

"No. I watched her talking to everyone after the helicopter left."

"Do you know if she's at the clinic?"

"I don't see her car parked along the side."

Panic added to his sense of doom. "Thanks, sweetheart." Derek immediately called the clinic, but no one answered. Next he phoned Sam Davis and discovered that Alex had just left his ranch and was on her way to the Moore ranch.

"What's the matter?" Beavins asked, walking back into the office, a cup of coffee in his hand.

"You know that guy we suspected of abusing steroids? Well, Simon brought him into the clinic today. Apparently the guy was so sick he had to be taken by helicopter to the hospital in Alpine."

"So?"

Derek explained the danger Randy faced.

"Still, I don't see what is so critical."

"I've got this nagging feeling that something's going down. I just don't know what." He stood and walked to the window. He tried calling Alex on the cellular phone, but the line was busy. "I think I'll drive out and see if I can intercept Alex before she gets to Simon's ranch.''

"But there's no evidence of anything going on.''

Derek paused by the door. "I've learned from hard experience to listen to my gut feeling.''

The mobile phone rang, making Alex jump. She answered it. "Hello.''

"Who's this?'' the male voice asked.

"Dr. Alexandra Courtland. Who are you?''

"Ah, Doc, sorry about that. This is Sheriff Wesley Clayton. I was trying to get in touch with Derek, and having a woman answer his mobile number was a shock.''

"Derek wanted me to use it while I was visiting several of the ranches.''

"Do you know where he is? I've tried his office and radio but don't get any answers.''

"He's at his ranch with Agent Beavins going over some information.''

"Thanks. By the way, I heard about the case you sent to Alpine.''

"How'd you hear about that?'' Alex asked.

"I was at the hospital when the chopper left. How's the guy doing?''

"Don't know. But I'm on my way to the Moore ranch now. The housekeeper called in a panic. Her son is running a fever and she asked me to come take a look at him. I'll check with the hospital when I get there.''

"Doctor, y—'' The phone connection crackled, then broke up.

"Hello, Sheriff, you there?''

Static filled her ear.

With a sigh she hung up. As she drove on, she wondered why Sheriff Clayton had sounded so odd before she lost him.

"Wait, Derek," Beavins yelled, racing out the front door. "The sheriff's on the phone. He needs to talk to you."

Derek sprinted inside. "Wes, what is it?"

"The NCIC computer just gave me five names of known dealers that Simon has called in the past six months. Jorge Martinez is on the top of the list."

Derek cursed. Jorge Martinez was a slippery little fish. He always managed to be around something illegal but was smart enough never to leave his fingerprints on anything. So far he'd been connected to half a dozen crimes, but the authorities on either side of the border never had enough evidence to charge him.

"DEA thinks he's up to his old tricks and are watching his house in El Paso. From phone records and surveillance, we can piece together that Jorge left his house immediately after Simon placed a call to him yesterday."

The knot in Derek's stomach tightened. "What kind of car does Jorge drive?"

"A recent-model green Jag." The sheriff gave the license plate number.

"Thanks, Wes."

"Derek, one other thing. When I was trying to get hold of you, I got Dr. Courtland on your mobile phone. She was on her way to the Moore ranch. I tried to warn her not to go, but the call broke up and I couldn't get her back."

Derek's original vague feeling of doom crystallized into bone-chilling fear. He knew in his heart that Alexandra was heading into trouble. "Wes, I'm going out to the Moore ranch now. I'll radio you for backup if I see Jorge's Jag."

Derek briefed Beavins on the conversation.

"Want me to go with you?" Beavins asked.

Derek nodded, and both men ran to Derek's Jeep. The engine roared to life and Derek floored the gas pedal, all the while praying he wouldn't be too late.

Alex parked her car behind a green Jaguar, which was parked behind Simon's Cadillac.

"Well, at least the man's at home," Alex muttered, "even if he does have company." Grabbing her bag, she climbed out of her car.

As she raised her hand to knock, she heard voices. Although she couldn't make out the individual words, the angry tones came through loud and clear. She hesitated only a moment before taking the brass knocker and banging it against the door.

The voices stopped and several moments later the door flew open. Simon Moore frowned at her. "What now, Doctor?"

Alex didn't much care for the man's surly tone, but she'd give him some leeway since he was still probably upset about Randy's condition and his own TB. "Mrs. Burns called and asked me to come by and see her son. Also, I need to read the test results of the other people here."

A maniacal light appeared in Simon's pale blue eyes. She'd seen that same look this past year in several of the soldiers' eyes when they had lost touch with reality.

"Yeah, Doc, come in. There's someone I want you to meet before you see the boy."

Alex took a step backward. Simon's arm whipped out and he grasped her upper arm. "This way, Doc."

He pulled her down the hall past the living room to a door on the opposite wall. Pushing it open, he dragged Alex behind him.

"Doc, I want you to meet another sick bastard. He knew he had TB. He quit taking his medicine, didn't you, Jorge?"

The man standing by the window appeared healthy at the moment. He flashed Simon a smile. "*Mi amigo,* the doctors don't know what they are talking about. I had the sickness, then took their medicine, and now I feel fine."

"How long ago were you diagnosed with TB?" Alex asked.

The man shrugged, seemingly unconcerned. "Six, seven months ago. I took the pills for a couple of months and now I am fine."

Alex glanced at Simon and prayed her alarm didn't show.

"He's the one who gave it to me, isn't he?" There was a sinister note in Simon's voice that made Alex's skin crawl.

"I can't say for sure."

Simon reached into the middle drawer of his desk and pulled out a .44 Magnum. Calmly he pointed it at Jorge. "Sure you can. I've spent a lot of time with Jorge here. We've been in real close quarters. And he's been coughing in my face the whole *damn* time."

Alex tried to keep all expression off her face, not wanting to give Simon any more reason to use his gun.

"Didn't you say that, Doc? That I could get TB from being in an enclosed space for a long time with someone who had it? Maybe like being cooped up in an airplane for hours with Jorge here.''

"You could've gotten it from Randy or Norma.''

"Randy works for Jorge. He's only been with me the last couple of weeks.''

Simon was, in his own sick way, pinning down the source of the TB bacteria. It made sense. Norma hadn't left Saddle for the past six months, so chances were that someone had infected her. And here stood her best suspect.

"You're wrong, my friend,'' Jorge said, edging toward the door.

"Don't move,'' Simon warned. "Doc, am I right? Is this the bastard who gave me the sickness?''

Alex hesitated. "I can't say.''

"See, she does not know,'' Jorge said.

Simon looked at her, and his feverish gaze searched hers.

The next thing Alex knew, Jorge was pulling a gun from under his sports jacket, but before he could pull the trigger, Simon fired. The force of the bullet slammed Jorge against the wall, and he slid to the floor.

Alex's gaze fixed on the blood staining the wall and she froze, unable to move or speak.

Derek didn't bother with the road that would have added ten to fifteen minutes to the trip. He cut straight across the flat land.

The direct line dumped them at the rear of Simon's house. Derek parked his Jeep behind a small shed that had been a smokehouse in earlier times, and the two men raced to the main house.

Derek and Beavins crouched down and worked their way along the side of the building. Halfway around they heard angry voices coming from a window above their heads. Racing forward, Derek found his worst fears confirmed when he peeked around the corner of the brick house and saw Jorge's green Jaguar, Simon's Cadillac and Alexandra's Mustang.

"Everyone's here," Beavins whispered.

"Yeah."

"I'll call for backup, then position myself by that back door I saw. Give me five minutes before you go in."

"All right," Derek answered.

As he watched Beavins work his way to the Jeep, Derek moved back to the window where he'd heard the voices. He could make out a few words. Simon was railing at Jorge and asking Alexandra questions. Then he heard a gunshot.

Alexandra! Derek's brain yelled. Instantly he was running. Terror chilled his blood as he imagined all sorts of horrors that could've happened to her. He grabbed his pistol from his holster and shoved open the front door.

The moment he stepped inside he saw the housekeeper, Mrs. Burns, rush into the hall. She froze and Derek motioned her back into the kitchen. After she left, he cautiously made his way down the hall.

"He deserved it." Simon's voice floated past the open library door.

Silence greeted his statement.

His heart racing, Derek slowly looked around the library door. Alex stood staring at the bloody wall. Simon hovered over the body sprawled on the floor;

he glanced up and saw Derek in the doorway. His hand shot out, yanking Alex to his side.

"Put the gun down, Simon," Derek ordered.

"No. And don't come any closer, because I'll hurt the doc here."

The vacant look in Alex's eyes worried Derek. "Alexandra," he softly called.

Simon's arm slid around her neck and he pressed the barrel of the gun to her temple. Something flickered in her eyes.

"Alexandra." Derek tried again to reach inside her panic and touch the rational part of her mind. Her eyes focused on him and he saw recognition return to the blue depths.

"Put the gun down, Derek, and move out of my way," Simon ordered. "Now." His arm flexed around Alex's neck.

Derek laid his gun on the edge of the desk. "Simon, there's no way you're going to escape. Just put down the weapon and everything will be okay."

"No, it won't. I'm not going to jail for shooting that scum. He deserved it. Now, if you don't get out of my way, I'll shoot the doc here."

Derek's gaze again met Alex's. As clearly as if she had spoken, Derek knew she was going to act, and he prepared himself.

"Move away from the gun," Simon shouted, waving his weapon, indicating for Derek to step back. Derek didn't move.

Simon tried to take a step toward the door, but Alex collapsed against him. Her deadweight caught him by surprise and he staggered forward. Derek lunged for his gun, aimed at Simon and fired.

At the same instant Simon pulled the trigger of his Magnum.

The noise reverberated in Alex's brain. She fought against the rising hysteria threatening her and concentrated on the sound in the room. Behind her, Simon was screaming; Derek lay on the floor before her, his teeth gritted against the pain of the wound in his upper thigh.

Alex picked up Simon's gun then glanced at him. He lay on his side, one hand clutching his upper arm. Pushing up Simon's short sleeve, she examined the flesh wound. He could wait.

She moved to Derek's side and knelt. Blood gushed between his fingers as he held his leg. A sense of urgency gripped her.

"Let me see," Alex commanded Derek.

The instant he moved his hand away, blood seeped through the fabric of his pant leg. With a strength born of an adrenaline surge, she put her fingers in the tiny bullet hole in the material and ripped. The amount of blood made it hard to see the entry point of the wound, but experience with gunshot wounds having this much blood dictated that Derek's articular artery, the main blood vessel in his thigh, had been nicked or severed. If she didn't put pressure on the wound, Derek would bleed to death in a matter of minutes.

"How bad is it?"

Alex glanced up and saw Beavins standing above her. "Get me something that I can use to put over his wound to stop the bleeding. A towel, a shirt, anything."

Alex placed her hand over the wound. Blood oozed between her fingers and seeped out under her palm.

"Here." Beavins shoved a towel in her face.

She grabbed it and put it over the wound, then pressed with all her might.

"I'm going to need that Medi-Vac copter here. Now. Derek doesn't have much time."

Beavins nodded and disappeared out of the room.

Derek tried to smile at her. "You seem to know what you're doing, Doc." His breathing was shallow, and he sounded out of breath.

"You forget, this is what I've been doing for the last few years."

"I trust you with my life." His eyes fluttered closed.

"Dammit, Derek Grey. Don't you give up on me."

Beavins entered the room. "The copter is on its way. What about the other two over here?"

Alex didn't bother to look at the other men. "Martinez is dead. Simon has a flesh wound, nothing serious."

Alex leaned her weight on the wound, praying that help would get here before Derek went into shock. His color was getting bad and when he opened his eyes, his pupils looked dilated.

It seemed like forever until she heard the chopper blades. A tear slipped from the corner of her eye as relief swept over her. If she had equipment, IVs, she could help Derek. Without it, all she could do was watch him die. "Tell the paramedics to hurry," Alex told Beavins. She leaned forward. "Help's here, Derek."

The corner of Derek's mouth kicked up, but his eyes remained closed. "It's always been here, Doc."

* * *

Alex leaned back against the wall outside surgery room one and closed her eyes. She was exhausted and emotionally wrung out.

"How'd it go, Dr. Courtland?"

Slowly Alex opened her eyes and saw Sheriff Wesley Clayton and Agent Beavins standing in the hall.

"It went fine. We were able to repair the artery and replace the fluid Derek had lost quickly enough that he should completely recover."

Beavins held out his hand. "I want to shake your hand, ma'am. You kept your head in a mighty explosive situation. Your clear thinking saved Derek's life."

The agent's words made Alex stop and think about what had happened. She realized she had acted quickly, without hesitation. Never once had she been other than focused on saving Derek's life. There had been no doubt about her competence or her skill. She had simply done what she had been trained to do. And if she was asked to do it again, she knew she could.

Alexandra took the man's hand. "Thank you."

The sheriff held out his hand. "I'd like to shake your hand, too."

Beavins leaned against the wall. "I also heard one of the nurses tell Dr. Shelly that you did a mighty fine piece of surgery."

A chuckle escaped. "I bet that made his day."

Beavins frowned. "He did have a peculiar look on his face, like he'd gotten hold of a sour pickle."

When they had wheeled Derek into the Alpine hospital, Dr. Shelly had told her he would do the repair surgery. But she had calmly informed him that because she had done countless emergency surgeries to repair blood vessels and organs during the past year, she had more experience in this area. And she would be the one to operate. Dr. Shelly had allowed her to do so, but hadn't bothered to hide his antagonism.

Besides, Alexandra had known she couldn't allow anyone else to work on Derek. She glanced down at her sweat-stained scrubs. "I'd better change." Of course, her clothes were in worse shape than these scrubs.

"Before you do, there's someone who wants to see you out in the parking lot," Beavins said.

"Who?"

"Why don't you go see?"

Beavins led Alex to the door where Sarah stood waiting in the cool night air with Todd and Cathy Grey. The instant the girl saw Alex she rushed from her aunt and uncle's side into Alex's arms.

Alex held her close.

"Is he going to be all right?" Sarah sobbed.

At that instant Alex knew that she had found the one place on the planet where she belonged. She also knew she had found her family. And she had found love.

Alex tilted Sarah's chin up. "Your dad is going to recover completely." She looked at Todd and Cathy. They both seemed to collapse with relief.

Sarah's chin quivered. "Thank you for saving him. I wish you would stay with us forever."

"Would you like that?"

Sarah's eyes widened. "Yes."

"I'll see what I can arrange."

Sarah squealed with joy. "I knew it."

Alex grinned at the girl's reaction.

"Can I see my dad?"

"Not now. You haven't been on your medication long enough for us to chance it. But I'll go check on him, and if he's awake, I'll have him wave to you from the window."

"Okay."

Alex motioned to Todd. "Why don't you come with me?"

They walked down the hall to the recovery room, only to discover Derek was still asleep. Watching Derek sleep peacefully, Alex turned to Todd. "You know that ad the folks of Saddle have been running for a doctor?"

"Yeah."

"You don't need to run it anymore. I'm applying for the position. Think there's any chance I'll get it?"

"I don't doubt it, Alex. You see, Derek is the one who's responsible for hiring."

Derek slowly opened his eyes and tried to make sense of his surroundings. His gaze traveled around the room until he saw Alexandra slumped in a chair beside the bed. The pain shooting up his leg reminded him of what had occurred. Simon Moore had shot him.

He remembered Alexandra's worried expression as she had hovered over him, pressing her weight against his aching thigh. But he had seen something else in her eyes that had warmed his heart. He had seen a concern so deep that if it wasn't love, it wouldn't take much more effort to turn it into love.

There were dark circles under Alex's eyes, and it appeared she hadn't had much rest over the past few hours. He reached out to touch her. The sound of the

IV tube in his arm bouncing off the metal stand mixed with her startled intake of breath.

"You're awake," she said, sitting up. She checked his IV, then looked into his eyes with her little flashlight. As she reached for the blood pressure cuff, he grabbed her wrist.

"Quit fussing."

She gave him a frosty look. "Who's the doctor here, Deputy?"

"All right." He surrendered his arm to her. He watched in amusement as she listened for his pressure and counted his heart beats.

"Do you give this kind of treatment to all your patients?"

She took her fingers away from his wrist. "No. I only give this kind of treatment to someone I love."

That shut him up. Dumbfounded, he stared at her.

He saw her fingers tremble as she fiddled with the stethoscope around her neck.

The door swung open and Wesley Clayton walked in. "You're awake. You gave us a mighty big scare, Derek."

"It didn't set well with me, either, Wes."

The sheriff grinned. "Well, I'll tell you, you lucked out. Your Dr. Courtland is the talk of the hospital, the way she took charge and operated on you. The lady's got some skilled hands."

Derek's gaze rested on Alexandra. He knew for a fact how skilled her hands were. "You operated yourself?"

She appeared uncomfortable with the praise. "Yes."

"Why didn't you let someone else do it?"

"I was more qualified." She tried to step away, but he caught her hand. The significance of what she'd done—saving his life—hit him like a moving freight train.

"How is Simon?"

"After his arm was bandaged, I put him under armed guard here at the hospital," Wes answered.

"Martinez?"

"Dead."

"Wes, I need a few moments alone with my doctor."

"Sure, Derek. I'll check back with you later today."

Once they were alone, Derek tugged Alex closer. "You said you loved me. Did you mean it?"

She looked as if she regretted having admitted to the emotion. She stared at the wall, swallowed, then looked him in the eye. "Yes."

He couldn't help the grin that spread across his face. "That is the sweetest word I've ever heard, Alexandra."

"What?"

"I've known for some time that I loved you, only I was too scared to tell you. Afraid I might run you off."

"That's what you were holding back?"

"Guilty."

"Oh, Derek, I thought you were trying to tell me you didn't want to get married again."

He captured her face between his hands.

"I want to marry you, Alexandra, and I want us to grow old together and watch our children have children. Do you want that, too? Do you want to have my children?"

"More than anything."

She leaned down and tenderly kissed him. When she tried to pull back, he slipped his hand behind her neck.

"I think Sarah's going to be pleased," he said between kisses.

"I already have her approval."

"You do?"

"I do. And I'd better warn you that I've already accepted the job as doctor for Saddle. You can quit looking."

Derek couldn't keep from grinning. "Sweetheart, I quit looking the moment I laid eyes on you."

* * * * *

▼INTIMATE MOMENTS®
™ Silhouette®

COMING NEXT MONTH

Take 4 bestselling love stories FREE

Plus get a FREE surprise gift!

Special Limited-time Offer

Mail to Silhouette Reader Service™

3010 Walden Avenue
P.O. Box 1867
Buffalo, N.Y. 14269-1867

YES! Please send me 4 free Silhouette Intimate Moments® novels and my free surprise gift. Then send me 6 brand-new novels every month, which I will receive months before they appear in bookstores. Bill me at the low price of $2.89 each plus 25¢ delivery and applicable sales tax, if any.* That's the complete price and a savings of over 10% off the cover prices—quite a bargain! I understand that accepting the books and gift places me under no obligation ever to buy any books. I can always return a shipment and cancel at any time. Even if I never buy another book from Silhouette, the 4 free books and the surprise gift are mine to keep forever.

245 BPA ANRR

Name	(PLEASE PRINT)	
Address	Apt. No.	
City	State	Zip

This offer is limited to one order per household and not valid to present Silhouette Intimate Moments® subscribers. *Terms and prices are subject to change without notice. Sales tax applicable in N.Y.

UMOM-295   ©1990 Harlequin Enterprises Limited

Become a Privileged Woman, You'll be entitled to all these Free Benefits. And Free Gifts, too.

To thank you for buying our books, we've designed an exclusive FREE program called *PAGES & PRIVILEGES™*. You can enroll with just one Proof of Purchase, and get the kind of luxuries that, until now, you could only read about.

Big Hotel Discounts

A privileged woman stays in the finest hotels. And so can you—at up to 60% off! Imagine standing in a hotel check-in line and watching as the guest in front of you pays $150 for the same room that's only costing you $60. Your *Pages & Privileges* discounts are good at Sheraton, Marriott, Best Western, Hyatt and thousands of other fine hotels all over the U.S., Canada and Europe.

Free Discount Travel Service

A privileged woman is always jetting to romantic places. When <u>you</u> fly, just make one phone call for the lowest published airfare at time of booking— <u>or double the difference back!</u>

PLUS—you'll get a $25 voucher to use the first time you book a flight AND <u>5% cash back on every ticket you buy thereafter through the travel service!</u>